*The Emperor's plan has been thwarted...
for now!*

But he has an even more
diabolical plot in store.

Can the Promethean Underground
prevent him from brainwashing
the entire city of Philadelphia?

Victor, Scott, and Jaime face their
greatest challenge yet, when

BENJAMIN FRANKLINSTEIN MEETS THOMAS DEADISON!

Also by
MATTHEW McELLIGOTT
& LARRY TUXBURY

BENJAMIN
FRANKLINSTEIN
LIVES!

Wherein is contained
an Accounting of the Preparation,
Suspension, and eventual Reawakening of the Subject in Modern Day,
and his Quest to discover the Great Emergency.

BENJAMIN FRANKLINSTEIN

MEETS THE

FRIGHT BROTHERS

BENJAMIN FRANKLINSTEIN MEETS THE FRIGHT BROTHERS

Wherein is contained
an Accounting of the Quest by our Subject
and his Young Compatriots to solve a Mystery of Vampires
terrorizing the Great City of Philadelphia.

By MATTHEW McELLIGOTT
& LARRY TUXBURY. PHILOM.

Illustrated by Matthew McElligott
Printed and fold by G. P. PUTNAM'S SONS
AN IMPRINT OF PENGUIN GROUP (USA) INC.
At the New Printing Office near the Market.

ACKNOWLEDGMENT

Jason Gough, meteorological wizard.

G. P. PUTNAM'S SONS · A DIVISION OF PENGUIN YOUNG READERS GROUP.
Published by The Penguin Group.
Penguin Group (USA) Inc., 375 Hudson Street, New York, NY 10014, U.S.A.
Penguin Group (Canada), 90 Eglinton Avenue East, Suite 700, Toronto, Ontario M4P 2Y3,
Canada (a division of Pearson Penguin Canada Inc.).
Penguin Books Ltd, 80 Strand, London WC2R 0RL, England.
Penguin Ireland, 25 St. Stephen's Green, Dublin 2, Ireland
(a division of Penguin Books Ltd.).
Penguin Group (Australia), 250 Camberwell Road, Camberwell, Victoria 3124,
Australia (a division of Pearson Australia Group Pty Ltd).
Penguin Books India Pvt Ltd, 11 Community Centre, Panchsheel Park,
New Delhi—110 017, India.
Penguin Group (NZ), 67 Apollo Drive, Rosedale, Auckland 0632, New Zealand
(a division of Pearson New Zealand Ltd).
Penguin Books (South Africa) (Pty) Ltd, 24 Sturdee Avenue, Rosebank,
Johannesburg 2196, South Africa.
Penguin Books Ltd, Registered Offices: 80 Strand, London WC2R 0RL, England.

Published simultaneously in Canada. Printed in the United States of America.
Design by Marikka Tamura and Annie Ericsson. Text set in ITC Cheltenham.
The art was done in a combination of traditional and digital techniques.

Library of Congress Cataloging-in-Publication Data
McElligott, Matthew.
Benjamin Franklinstein meets the Fright brothers / by Matthew McElligott and Larry
Tuxbury. p. cm.—(Benjamin Franklinstein ; 2) Summary: Victor and his friends, aided
by Benjamin Franklin, uncover an evil scheme involving giant bats and two mysterious
brothers, and learn more about the secretive Modern Order of Prometheus.
1. Franklin, Benjamin, 1706–1790—Juvenile fiction. [1. Franklin, Benjamin, 1706–1790—
Fiction. 2. Scientists—Fiction. 3. Secret societies—Fiction.] I. Tuxbury, Larry. II. Title.
PZ7.M478448Bn 2011 [Fic]—dc22 2010040431
ISBN 978-0-399-25480-2

3 5 7 9 10 8 6 4

For Christy and Anthony, and especially to Larry,
wordsmith extraordinaire. —M.M.

For Melanie, Nina, and Ella.
Also for Matt, a great judge of talent. —L.T.

And for Tim, the spark that
brought Ben to life. —M.M. & L.T.

"Fear not death;
for the sooner we die,
the longer shall we be immortal."

—Benjamin Franklin

FREQUENTLY ASKED QUESTIONS
about Benjamin Franklinstein

Is Benjamin Franklin still alive?

Yes.

How is that possible?

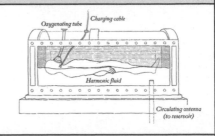

Centuries ago, Franklin and a group of scientists called the *Modern Order of Prometheus* invented the Leyden casket. It preserved Franklin for over two hundred years.

What was the mission of the Modern Order of Prometheus?

Its mission was to preserve the world's greatest scientists, awakening them when the world needed them most.

Where was Franklin preserved?

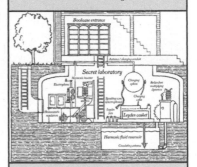

In a secret basement laboratory beneath a house in Philadelphia. This house is currently owned by *Mary Godwin* and her son, Victor.

Who took care of Franklin while he slept?

For centuries, a series of Custodians of the Order watched over Franklin's sleeping body. But several months ago, his last Custodian, Mr. Mercer, died unexpectedly, leaving Franklin unattended.

So what woke up Franklin?

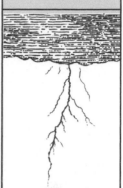

Apparently, a freak lightning strike on an otherwise cloudless evening.

Who knows that Franklin is alive?

Only Victor Godwin, the boy who lives in the apartment above Franklin's, knows his secret. Victor has been helping Franklin adjust to life in the twenty-first century,

Was Benjamin Franklin the only scientist preserved by the Modern Order of Prometheus?

No...

PROLOGUE
Philadelphia, 1948

It had taken a long time for the elevator to stop. Orville shivered. As a man accustomed to soaring high above the earth, he found it unsettling to be so deep beneath it.

His fingers traced the fresh scar on his temple.

"You will soon grow used to the harmonium plate," said the short man in the neat suit standing beside him. "Consider yourself lucky. In the Order's early days, the electrical contacts were not hidden beneath the skin. Instead, our scientists had crude bolts implanted into their necks."

"Either way," scoffed Orville, "I feel like a machine."

The short man smiled as he pulled open the safety gate. He waved a hand, gesturing for Orville to exit.

Orville stepped into a cavernous laboratory filled with pulsating, electrified equipment.

"Good lord, Enbée," he said, gawking up at the colossal machine in the center. "What is it?"

"That, *mon ami,*" the short man replied, "is our Tesla coil. The great Serbian scientist Nikola Tesla designed it especially for the Modern Order of Prometheus, just before he went into his own deep sleep five years ago."

Orville circled the device, awestruck. "What does it do?"

"It is our power source," Monsieur Enbée said. "It is capable of producing electrical vibrations in excess of one hundred million volts. Think of it, Mr. Wright: *man-made lightning.*"

The Tesla coil towered over them. A pole wrapped in tightly wound wire reached up twenty feet and was capped near the ceiling by a great metal dome. A circular metal cage surrounded the pole to prevent the foolhardy from stepping too close.

On either side of the Tesla coil lay large caskets, one open, one closed. Orville trudged to the closed casket and put his hand on it. It was made of a thick glass bound by strips of steel. Inside, he could make out a shadowy shape floating in a glowing blue liquid. A soft blip sounded from a speaker mounted on its side.

Orville peered into the glass and gazed upon the face he had not seen in over thirty-five years.

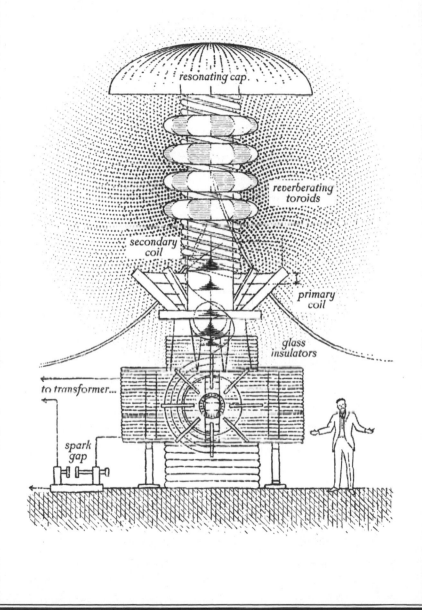

resonating cap.

reverberating
toroids

secondary
coil

primary
coil

glass
insulators

to transformer...

spark
gap

"Brother," he whispered.

"My friend," Monsieur Enbée said, "I am pleased that you have at last agreed to join the Order."

Orville frowned. "At this point, what do I have to lose? My heart is weak. Whether I climb into that terrible box or not, I'm likely to die."

"Have faith," Monsieur Enbée said, looking up into the frail man's eyes. "True, you have resisted for decades. Not like your brother. Ah, his enthusiasm for the Order was intoxicating!"

"I remember," Orville said. "It was a lifetime ago. We were both young, but his spirit of adventure was much bolder than mine." Wright looked sharply at the short man. "I'm curious, Enbée. The last time we both stood in this room was thirty-six years ago, when Wilbur joined your secret society. Since then, I have grown old and weak. You, however—you haven't aged a day. How can that be?"

"Witness the scientific marvels around you," the short man proclaimed. "We have the technology to make a man live indefinitely. Does it not make sense that I, as director of the Order, extend my own life span? I am older than you think. And just as your brother and I have benefited from these miracles of science, so will you."

Despite Monsieur Enbée's reassuring words, there was something about him that Orville didn't trust. "But you promise," Orville insisted, waving a finger at the Leyden caskets. "You promise that when we awaken, we shall awaken together."

Monsieur Enbée smiled thinly. "*Mais, bien sûr . . .* of course. If ever the world faces a great emergency, history's finest scientists and inventors will all be awakened to come to its rescue. That is the purpose of the Modern Order of Prometheus, as determined by our founder, Benjamin Franklin."

Benjamin Franklin, Orville thought. *There was a great man.*

"But what of my family?" pressed Orville. "And the affairs of my life?"

"All has been arranged. Your family will be well cared for, and the details of your 'funeral' are already in place. I assure you, we take good care of our own." He put his hand on Orville's shoulder. "Trust me, Mr. Wright. Trust the Order."

Orville nodded. "Very well. What must I do?"

"We shall leave it to your Custodian." He gestured to a tall man who waited silently behind the open Leyden casket. Orville had not noticed him standing there. "He will perform the suspension-of-life procedure."

The Custodian led Orville up a small step to the casket, assisting him into the blue liquid. The fluid immediately began to glow. The Custodian gently fitted a rubber mask over the old man's mouth and nose.

"Do not worry," the Custodian said. "I am told it is like sleep. You and your brother will be reunited, one day. And it will seem as only an instant."

Orville looked at his brother's casket. It had been so many years. So many decades. He sighed, closed his eyes, and lowered the rest of his body into the fluid. The Custodian closed the lid and sealed the latch. Air bubbles rose to the top of the casket. Orville Wright was breathing normally.

The Custodian flicked a switch, and the steady rhythm of Orville's heartbeat blipped from a speaker. He gripped a lever and pushed it up. The Tesla coil hummed. At first it gave off a low, soft buzz, but within seconds the noise grew louder, more high-pitched, deafening.

Sparks wheeled off from the coil at the center. Suddenly, the room was awash in bolts of lightning that sliced the air, crackling from the dome at the top. Ribbons of raw energy flashed, racing around the cage. The Leyden caskets were bathed in electricity. Monsieur Enbée and the Custodian shielded their eyes.

An alarm blared from the control panel, and red lights flashed a warning.

"Quick!" shouted Monsieur Enbée. "Stabilize the neutron flow!"

The Custodian reached for the lever but snapped his hand back, howling in pain. "It's hypercharged!"

He flung open a cabinet and snatched out two vulcanized rubber gloves. "Stand back, Monsieur Enbée!"

The small man retreated into a corner as the Custodian gripped the lever and pulled down with his full weight. Slowly, it descended. As it did, the lightning that had filled the room drew back into the Tesla coil. The crackle and hum of pure energy softened and then vanished.

The Custodian pounded a large button with his fist. The flashing red lights and buzzing ceased. He removed his goggles and gloves. "It's safe. We've reached bioelectric homeostasis."

Monsieur Enbée slowly approached Orville Wright's Leyden casket. "Did it work? I'm not hearing a heartbeat. The Order cannot afford to lose another one."

"Wait," the Custodian said.

They waited. Ten seconds . . . twenty seconds . . . thirty seconds . . .

Blip! . . . Blip! . . .

"Ah," Monsieur Enbée said, with a sigh of relief. "He lives."

"But we almost lost him," the Custodian said. "I warned you, Enbée. Tesla's machine is dangerous."

"You just keep him alive," the short man snapped back. "As long as I am in charge, it is not your place to question the Order's methods."

"Yes, sir. My apologies, sir."

The small man stepped into the elevator and pushed the button. "And in the future, you will remember to refer to me as *Monsieur* Enbée. *Comprenez-vous?*"

"Yes, Monsieur Enbée," the Custodian said. "I understand."

The doors closed on the small man. The elevator began to grind its way to the surface.

"Know your place, Custodian," called Monsieur Enbée, "and remember your duty. I have put great trust in you!"

Then why, the Custodian thought, *do I find it so difficult to trust you?*

IMPERIAL COAT OF ARMS OF FRANCE (EARLY 19TH CENTURY)

CHAPTER ONE
Philadelphia, Today

It was a typical, sunny summer afternoon on Karloff Avenue. A woman was watering the plants in her garden. A mailman was making his daily rounds. Two mothers with strollers chatted on the sidewalk.

And high above them, balanced precariously on the chimney of the oldest house on the block, Benjamin Franklin was disco dancing while mooing like a cow.

Had anyone on the street happened to look up, it is unlikely they would have recognized the great American patriot. He wore Bermuda shorts, a tattered T-shirt, and a scarf to disguise the strange metal bolts in his neck. He danced vigorously, although there was no music playing. Two sparking electrical cables were clipped to the garters on his tall black socks. The cables ran to a rusty old machine, which was being carefully monitored by a boy sitting on a wooden crate.

Fortunately, no one on the street happened to look up. If they had, they would surely have called the police.

"Point your left hand a little more to the west," called Victor. He studied a gauge. "I'm certain we've found the right frequency. Maybe the signal strength is still too low? Try humming again."

"Moooooooooo . . ."

"Can you hum louder? And really swing your hips back and forth this time. We need to get you in phase with the chromatic overtones."

Franklin nodded and intensified his dance. The wires on his socks began to crackle and flash.

"MOOOOOOOOOOOOOOOOO! MOOOOOOOOOOOO!"

Victor watched the needles on the gauge swing back and forth. "That helps. Can you sense anything yet?"

Franklin huffed and shook his head. *"MOOOOOOOOO! . . . Nothing . . . MOOOOOO . . . at . . . MOOOOOO . . . all . . ."*

"Maybe if you—"

BOOM!

A bright blue flash lit the air, followed by a puff of dark black smoke. The old man tumbled off the chimney onto the roof below.

Victor raced to Franklin's side. "Ben, are you okay?"

Franklin blinked and slowly pulled himself upright. "I'm fine," he said. "Never better."

"What happened?"

"Exactly what I feared might happen." He nodded down toward his feet, where two black rings now encircled his bare ankles. "My socks exploded."

"Yikes! I'm sorry."

"Nonsense. They were old socks. Besides, your idea was sound. What better antenna for the electrophone than my own harmonically charged body? It was a brilliant insight."

"I was so sure we were on to something. Your movements gave us great reception, and when you hummed, the resonance indicator went all the way to full. I don't understand why we didn't pick up some sort of signal."

Franklin stood and dusted himself off. "Victor, I'm afraid the evidence is clear. There is no signal. We are alone."

"I don't agree."

"We have to face facts. The electrophone is the only way to contact any remaining members of the Modern Order of Prometheus. If no one is answering, then it can mean only one thing: the Order is no more."

"We don't know that for sure." Victor walked to the edge of the roof. "Look, you were asleep in the basement for over two hundred years. Then, a few weeks ago, out of the blue, something suddenly woke you up. Why?"

"What woke me was nothing more than a random strike of lightning."

"That's one possibility. Another is that the Modern Order of Prometheus woke you because they need your help. Maybe whenever they've tried to contact you, we just haven't been around."

"It has been a month," said Franklin. He stood beside Victor, watching the people go about their business on the street below. "We have monitored the electrophone regularly, in every possible way, and have yet to receive a single transmission."

Victor turned his gaze toward the Philadelphia skyline. "You're right. I know that. But I'm not ready to give up yet. I can't explain why."

Franklin smiled. "Victor, that doesn't sound very scientific. And from you, of all people!"

Victor's face reddened. "It's just, you know, a gut feeling."

"Then we press on. If there is one thing I believe in, it is following my gut. Speaking of which, how about something to eat?"

Downstairs in the Godwin apartment, Victor fixed some snacks in the kitchen while Franklin turned on the TV.

"Remind me again," Franklin called. "Where do I find the channel with the moving drawings?"

Recently, television had become Franklin's obsession. What surprised Victor were the types of programs Franklin chose to watch. He found C-SPAN, the news, and the History Channel interesting, but what he really loved were cartoons.

"Try channel thirty-two."

Victor could hear Franklin cursing at the remote in the other room. "The blasted television wand is broken again!"

"Have you pushed the On button?"

The television clicked on. "Never mind, I repaired it!" Franklin hollered.

Victor emptied the microwave popcorn into a bowl and poured two glasses of honey lemonade. When he entered the living room, Franklin was watching an anchorman on the local news.

"And now for the weather. Skip, how are things looking for tomorrow? Can we count on a sunny Fourth of July?"

"Oh, hurrah!" exclaimed Franklin. "It's Skip Weaver! I wonder what sort of tomfoolery he has in store this time."

Victor sighed. For better or for worse, Skip's son, Scott Weaver, was the closest thing he had to a friend at Philo T. Farnsworth Middle School. Scott never seemed to take anything very seriously, and his dad was the same way. Victor, on the other hand, took everything seriously.

On the television, Skip Weaver rode a scooter back and forth in front of the weather map. A cardboard pizza box emblazoned with a crude Magic Marker drawing of the sun was taped to the handlebars. On the screen behind him, animated storm clouds ran for their lives.

"The sun is chasing the clouds away!" howled Franklin. "Have you ever seen such a spectacle?"

Victor rolled his eyes.

Suddenly, the pizza box fell from the front of Skip's scooter and caught in the wheel. Skip lost control and skidded directly toward the camera. Something heavy crashed to the floor and the entire newsroom seemed to tip on its side. The screen went black, and the station cut to a used car commercial.

"Bravo!" cheered Franklin. "Bravo! Oh, it's pure genius!"

"It's embarrassing," said Victor. "If I want to see a clown, I'll go to the circus."

"Victor, that's Scott's father! Show some respect."

Victor snorted. "Watching his forecast is like watching a cartoon."

"My cartoons!" Franklin blurted. "Now where did I place that wand?" He reached beneath the seat cushion and rummaged for the remote. The commercial ended and the news came back on.

"Coming up, we'll take a look at those new electricity-free miracle lightbulbs that have been showing up in stores throughout the city. Do they really work? We'll find out! But first, we join Mayor Milstead's press conference, already in progress."

Mayor Milstead stood behind a podium, with two men

beside her. The first man wore a crisp blue suit and appeared to be standing at attention. The second man was much shorter. He slouched, and his beard was full of crumbs. The mayor began to speak.

"I am here today to talk about reports we have received of what some are calling giant monster bats flying over Philadelphia. In fact, some citizens have even called my office suggesting these may be vampires. Clearly, this is an overreaction to something that no doubt has a simple explanation. Still, I assure you that we take this issue very seriously . . ."

"A female mayor?" marveled Franklin. "Fascinating!"

"I've asked two authorities, Gilbert Girard from the Federal Aviation Administration and Dr. Robert Kane of the Philadelphia Zoo, to head up a special investigation. They will report directly to my office. In the meantime, we have established a toll-free hotline . . ."

"Oh, yeah, I read about this," said Victor. "Enormous bats flying around the city? It's preposterous."

"A short time ago, I would have told you that instant pudding was preposterous," said Franklin. "How can you be so certain?"

"Trust me."

"So there are no giant bats? No . . . vampires?"

"Of course not," said Victor. "It's probably just a publicity stunt. We don't have giant bats in Philadelphia, and there's no such thing as vampires."

THAT NIGHT...

Glenda Milstead, mayor of Philadelphia, poured herself a cup of tea and carried it out to the patio. A long day at City Hall had left her with a bad headache, and she needed to relax. She settled into her deck chair and gazed at the night sky.

It was dusk, and the stars were just beginning to emerge. Overhead, a bat flitted by, followed by two more. She watched them zigzag across the sky, chasing insects too small to see.

Bats. The last thing she wanted to think about.

All day long, her office had fielded more reports of giant bat sightings. Just this morning there had been almost *sixty* calls. Hopefully, the investigation would yield results. Something strange was definitely going on, and she planned to get to the bottom of it.

A soft rustling sound came from the bushes.

"Who's there?" Mayor Milstead called.

Silence.

The wind whispered and shook the trees.

Mayor Milstead let out a long sigh. All this talk of giant bats had her spooked. She turned to head back inside, then paused. Something still didn't feel right.

Fwooooooooosh!

Mayor Milstead felt a sharp bite on the side of her neck.

CHAPTER TWO
A Simple Solution

Wednesday was the Fourth of July. Victor rose bright and early and suddenly knew exactly what he had to do. It was an idea so simple, so obvious, he couldn't understand why he hadn't thought of it before.

There was no way Victor and Ben could be around twenty-four hours a day to listen for a call from the electrophone. But . . . they could *invent something* to do the listening for them. An alert system.

Still in his underwear, Victor raced to his desk and began to sketch some ideas. He knew the electrophone had a distinctive electrical charge when it was in use. All they'd need to do would be to attach a simple sensor to the pickup coil, and that sensor could connect to his laptop, and the laptop could send an alert to his phone . . .

One by one, the pieces snapped into place. The idea was simplicity itself. And with Ben's help, they might even be able to get it up and running before the parade started. Victor threw on some clothes and grabbed his laptop.

Downstairs, he knocked on the front door of Franklin's apartment. It was early, and there was a good chance the old man was still asleep. But this idea was so good, Victor was certain his friend wouldn't mind being disturbed.

Technically, Franklin didn't sleep. Whereas a normal person's body was more than half water, Franklin's coursed with electrified harmonic fluid, a wondrous substance that had allowed him to survive for centuries in suspended animation.

Unfortunately, the harmonic fluid lost its charge fairly quickly, so Franklin spent his nights plugged into an outlet in his apartment. This recharged both his bloodstream and the special battery belt that Victor had devised to keep him regulated through the day. Without the belt, Franklin risked becoming over- or underpowered, either of which could lead to disastrous results.

Victor knocked again, and the door swung open. There stood Franklin, proudly resplendent in his colonial-era clothing.

"Victor! Good morning!"

"Hi, Ben. I'm sorry to get you up so early."

"Early? I've been up for hours. Are you as excited about

the Independence Day Bicycle Parade as I am?"

"Uh, probably not as excited as you are," said Victor, "but, sure, I'm excited."

"You *must* see my bicycle. Please, come in."

Victor stepped inside Franklin's apartment. There, in the center of the room, stood the most ridiculously patriotic bike Victor had ever seen. Painted in alternating stripes of red, white, and blue, it sported streamers, cardboard stars, and a flag of Franklin's own "Don't Tread on Me" design. Even the tires had been decorated with glitter and stickers.

Franklin walked over and stood proudly beside the handlebars. "What do you think, my boy?"

"It's very . . . American. Did you do this all yourself?"

"I've been working on it all week. Is it enough?"

"Enough?"

"Enough to honor this great day! I have more stickers—"

"No, I think it has enough stickers," said Victor. "You've really been looking forward to this, haven't you?"

"Since seventeen seventy-six, my boy! I only wish Jefferson, Adams, and Washington could be here to share it with me. Well, maybe not Adams—he could get cranky. But you know what I mean."

"I do." Victor knelt down and admired Franklin's handiwork. "It's a great bike, Ben. I wouldn't change a thing."

"Thank you, Victor. And how are things with you?"

"Excellent. I've had a brainstorm."

Victor explained his plan for an electrophone alert system as Franklin listened intently. Although the old man had missed the last two centuries of technology, he was a quick study.

"It's brilliant!" said Franklin. He paused for a moment, deep in thought. "But . . . have you considered attaching the sensor *directly* to the speaking cone on the electrophone? That's where the harmonic signal strength should be greatest."

"I considered that," said Victor. "But wouldn't it interfere with the—"

"Not if we insulate the pickup coil completely," interrupted Franklin. "In fact, the insulation might well—"

"—solve our harmonic interference problem!" finished Victor. "It makes perfect sense. But we'd better hurry. Scott said he'd be here at nine thirty."

"To the laboratory!" announced Franklin, with a flourish.

The work went even faster than Victor had expected, and within an hour they had their alert system working pretty well. Victor went outside to wait for Scott while Franklin put a few finishing touches on his bicycle.

At ten fifteen, Victor finally spotted his friend pedaling around the corner at the far end of the street. He was carrying something big on his handlebars, and his bike wobbled and swerved under the weight. As he grew closer,

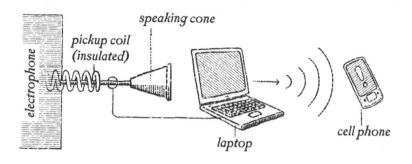

electrophone

pickup coil
(insulated)

speaking cone

laptop

cell phone

Victor could see that the object was a large, wooden antique radio.

"Hey, Victor," huffed Scott, "check it out. This used to . . . be my . . . grandfather's." Scott careened up the sidewalk, where he and the bike dropped, exhausted, onto their sides. The radio tumbled off the handlebars and onto the lawn.

Victor walked over and tipped the radio upright. It was the size of a picnic cooler, and fancier than most of the furniture in his house. "Nice. Does it still work?"

"Not so much," said Scott. "I thought I could fix it, but I think I just made it worse."

Victor pulled open a small door on the back of the radio. Inside was a tangle of dusty tubes and wires. "What have you tried?"

"All sorts of things," said Scott. "I noticed some of the

wires were red and some were black, so I colored them all black, but that didn't help. My dad said it wasn't safe to plug it in, so I added a bunch of batteries and wedged some aluminum foil into the empty spaces. The radio makes clucking sounds now, like there's a chicken in there. That's not right, is it?"

"Probably not," agreed Victor.

"So anyway, I was thinking that maybe I could leave it here and your uncle Frank could help me look at it. He's at least as old as the radio. Maybe he'll catch something I missed."

"We can ask him," said Victor, "although I don't know if—"

"Did someone mention my name?" Franklin appeared from around the side of the house, wheeling his star-spangled bike. To Victor's amazement, it was now covered with even more red, white, and blue decorations.

"Hey, Mr. Benjamin," called Scott. "That looks amazing!"

Franklin beamed. "Why, thank you, Scott. I am honored that you approve."

"I wish my bike looked like that. Don't you, Victor?"

"Uh, sure. Yes, of course I do."

"I have more stickers," offered Franklin. "Would you boys like some for your bikes?"

"That would be *awesome*," said Scott.

"Definitely," agreed Victor, "but I'm, uh . . . afraid we're out of time. You guys don't want to be late, do you?"

CHAPTER THREE
The Independence Day Bicycle Parade

The Independence Day bike parade was a patriotic spectacle. Hundreds of Philadelphians pedaled down the street on decorated bicycles. Mayor Milstead led the way, her own bike sporting a pair of lit sparklers on the handlebars. A local high school band had loaded their drums, trumpets, trombones, and even a sousaphone onto their bikes and played a clumsy but rousing rendition of "Stars and Stripes Forever."

A crowd cheered from the sidewalks, giving an extra ovation to a man dressed as Benajmin Franklin. He wore authentic eighteenth-century clothes as he wobbled along. Even with training wheels, his balance was uncertain.

"How's it going, Ben?" Victor asked, pedaling alongside.

"I admit to having some difficulty maintaining for-ward locomotion, steering, and sustaining my balance," Franklin huffed. "But experience is the best teacher, and I shall soon master this remarkable contraption!"

"Try not to think too much," Scott suggested. "That's what I do. Hey, look at that!"

A small airplane flew overhead, towing an enormous banner reading FREE BICYCLE REPAIRS AT THE RIGHT CYCLE CO.

Franklin grinned broadly, craning his neck to get a good look. "The airplane! Of all your modern-day inventions, that may be the most miraculous. I remember watching the Montgolfier brothers' first hot-air balloon flight. We never dreamed that it would lead to—"

"Watch the road!" Victor shouted.

Franklin swerved and narrowly avoided crashing into a cycling trombonist.

Several near misses later, the procession reached the performance stage in the park. Mayor Milstead got off her bike and joined four men who were waiting on the stage. A cluster of news vans was parked nearby, their cameras focused on the mayor.

"Citizens of Philadelphia," Mayor Milstead began, *"I would like to thank you all for participating in our first an-nual Independence Day Bicycle Parade."*

The crowd applauded.

Victor craned his neck. "I can't see anything. What's happening up there?"

"Yeah," Scott said. "I heard there was free ice cream somewhere."

"We're too far away," Franklin said. "Perhaps these will help."

He reached into his pocket and produced what looked like a small pair of binoculars. They were constructed of two empty toilet paper rolls, a number of hand-ground lenses, and some duct tape. "I've been experimenting with the science of optics and thought this might come in handy. I call it the bioptiscope."

Victor put them up to his eyes, and the mayor's face came into focus. "Wow, these work great."

"First," Mayor Milstead continued, gesturing to two men standing behind her, *"let us give a warm welcome to our city's two newest entrepreneurs, the proprietors of the Right Cycle Company. They have sponsored this wonderful bicycle parade. Would either of you like to say a few words?"*

After a smattering of applause, the younger of the two men stepped before the microphone. He was tall, thin, and extremely pale, dressed entirely in black from his shoes all the way up to his bowler hat. Victor thought his clothes looked old-fashioned, like something you might see in a silent movie. Even though the man wore sunglasses, he still shielded his eyes from the sun's rays with his hand. *"In appreciation of your show of patriotism, my brother and I are pleased to offer every single person in this parade, and anyone watching at home, a free bicycle tune-up this*

Saturday at our shop, the Right Cycle Company."

Everyone cheered.

Brothers? Victor wondered. One of them had to be at least thirty years older than the other. Peculiar.

Mayor Milstead took back the microphone. *"Thank you all. And now I have another announcement."*

"Do you notice anything odd about their speech?" Ben asked.

"They're all talking kind of slowly, almost like robots," said Victor. "Maybe they're nervous."

Franklin nodded. "Public speaking is a challenge for many. I remember when Patrick Henry first attempted to speak before the House of Burgesses. His voice squeaked so loudly that the entire House erupted into—"

"Hey, Victor," Scott interrupted, "can I try Mr. Benjamin's biopti-things? I want to get a better look."

"Sure." Victor handed them over.

Up on the stage, the mayor welcomed two more men to the podium. The first wore a crisp blue suit and appeared to be standing at attention. The second man was much shorter. He slouched and his beard was full of crumbs.

"Over the past few weeks," Mayor Milstead continued, *"there has been some concern regarding sightings of giant monster bats flying above the city. To clarify, I'd like to introduce Mr. Gilbert Girard of the Federal Aviation Administration Flight Standards District Office."*

The man in the blue suit leaned into the microphone.

"After exhaustive observation and research, the FAA conclusively reports that the bats that people claim to have seen are in fact mirages caused by swamp gas rising from the outskirts of town."

The crowd murmured.

"Thank you, Mr. Girard," Mayor Milstead said. *"We also have with us Dr. Robert Kane, eminent small-mammal zoologist from the Philadelphia Zoo. Dr. Kane, would you share your findings with the people of Philadelphia?"*

Dr. Kane took the microphone. *"After exhaustive observation and research, the Philadelphia Zoo conclusively reports that the bats that people claim to have seen are in fact mirages caused by swamp gas rising from the outskirts of town."*

"Do we even have swamps in Philadelphia?" Victor asked. "I thought —"

Beep! Beep! Beep!

"The transmitter!" Victor gasped, checking the readout on his cell phone. "Someone's calling on the electrophone!"

"We must return to the laboratory at once," Franklin said. "Follow me."

"Hey, guys," Scott said, peering through Franklin's bioptiscope, "there's something wrong with this thing. It makes the people up there look like they have glowing eyes."

He glanced around, but Victor and Franklin were gone. "Guys? Where'd you go?"

CHAPTER FOUR
A Voice from the Ether

Victor wove through the crowd, pedaling furiously. Ben struggled along behind, trying desperately to control his bike. In frustration, he hopped off and began to push.

"Go on without me, Victor!"

The phone was still beeping, but Victor knew it might stop at any second. What if the caller gave up and never called back? Victor's legs burned, but he pedaled faster.

At the corner, he made a split-second decision and jumped his bike up and over the curb. The path down the hill was dangerously steep, but it could save precious seconds. His bike shook as it bounced down the rutted incline. Victor found himself moving faster than he could pedal, and threw his weight from side to side in a desperate effort to steer. The front wheel wrenched to the right, and he toppled over the handlebars onto the hard ground.

The phone stopped beeping.

Victor's shoulder throbbed. Blood ran down his shin from his knee, but he scarcely noticed. He pulled the phone from his pocket and was relieved to see that the impact had only knocked the battery loose. Maybe the caller *hadn't* hung up. There might still be time.

The front rim of his bike was twisted at a right angle. He'd have to leave it behind. Victor raced, half running, half limping, toward the gap in the fence.

By the time he reached his house, he was in a full panic. He fumbled frantically with the keys and unlocked the door to Ben's downstairs apartment. Dashing to the back room, he pulled open the bookcase and clambered down the ladder into the secret basement laboratory.

He hit the floor hard, and his bloody knee buckled beneath him. Pain shot up his leg, and Victor, to his own surprise, screamed a swearword—the same word that sent Denny Burkus to the principal's office at least once a week.

"Hello? Dr. Franklin? Is that you?"

The electrophone—it was working!

Victor stumbled across the lab, sidestepping Franklin's Leyden jars on his way to the giant machine in the corner. He unrolled the electrophone's speaking tube and held the copper cone to his mouth.

"Hello!" Victor sputtered. "Who is this?"

He waited but heard no response.

"Hello?" Victor repeated. "Ben—I mean *Dr. Franklin* is on his way. Please don't hang up!"

"Who are you?" the voice cautiously inquired.

Victor couldn't tell whether the voice belonged to a man or a woman. The sound crackled and warbled, like an old record being played underwater.

"My name is Victor Godwin. I live in the house upstairs. I've been helping Dr. Franklin repair the electrophone. I promise, he'll be here any second."

"How do I know you're not . . . one of them?"

"One of them? One of who?"

"Don't even think of trying to trace this signal. I'll send you halfway around the world before I let you find me."

"Look," said Victor, "I don't know what you're talking about, but you can trust me. Ben told me all about the Modern Order of Prometheus. You're the reason he woke up, aren't you? So he could help you with a great emergency?"

"What do you know about the Great Emergency?"

So there really was one!

"I only know that Ben was supposed to sleep until the Prometheans needed him to help with something really big. He thinks he was revived by accident, but I knew there was more to it."

"Are you acting as his Custodian?"

"In a way. I've been helping him out."

"Where is he now? Is he in danger? Are you keeping him hidden?"

"He's, uh, on his way home from the bike parade."

"The parade! You let him be seen at the parade? Is he in disguise?"

"Sort of. He's dressed as Benjamin Franklin. It works better than you might think here in Philadelphia."

"You've put everything at risk! I dare not talk any longer. They may be listening."

"Wait!" said Victor. "Don't hang up! What's wrong with the parade? And what's the Great Emergency?"

"Study the news footage from the parade. I will make contact again when it is safe. And when I do, I expect to speak directly with Dr. Franklin."

The electrophone went dead.

Ben arrived several minutes later, flushed and out of breath.

"Victor, I am sorry, but that bicycle! I don't think it likes me." He stepped off the ladder and glanced across the room at the electrophone. "Were we too late?"

"I made it just in time, but I'm afraid it's bad news." He filled Franklin in.

For the first time since Victor met him, the old man seemed genuinely shaken.

"I have been a fool, Victor. Worse, I have been derelict in

my duties as a Promethean. I should have worked harder to contact the Order. Had it not been for your persistence—"

"It was a one-in-a-million shot," said Victor. "The important thing now is figuring out what to do about it. What do you think the voice meant when it asked if I was 'one of them'?"

"I do not know. But we must try to call back."

"I'm not so sure," Victor said. "The voice seemed afraid, as if speaking on the electrophone for too long was dangerous. It mentioned that someone else might be listening in."

"Then perhaps we, too, should stop trying for now," agreed Franklin. "The longer we broadcast, the more we may be putting ourselves in danger."

"That's a good point," said Victor. "I hope we haven't already—"

He stopped suddenly and tipped his head to the side. "Do you hear something?"

Someone was upstairs in Franklin's apartment.

"Did you lock the door?" whispered Victor.

Franklin winced. "I'm afraid I didn't even close it."

"And the bookcase? Is it still open?"

"Yes."

The footsteps grew louder.

"How could they find us so fast?" whispered Victor.

"Who?"

"*Them!* The ones listening in."

"Quick, the lights!"

Victor hit the switch, leaving only the dim blue glow of the Leyden jars to light the room. He and Franklin crouched behind the workbench, peering over the top. Across the room, a silhouette of one foot, then another, stepped down the ladder.

Victor tensed as he tried to form a plan. Should he throw something? Create a distraction? His heart pounded in his chest.

The shadowy form looked oddly familiar. It paused at the bottom rung.

"Hey, guys, are you down here? I brought back your biopti-thing. Whooooah . . . this place is cool!"

For the second time that day, Victor said a very bad word.

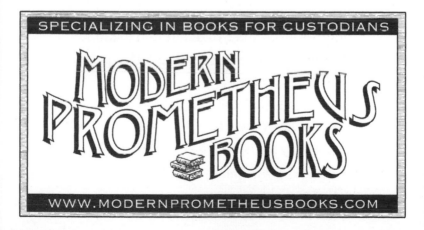

CHAPTER FIVE

A Secret Revealed

"Hold on a minute. Let's go through this one more time," Scott said. "You're telling me that Mr. Benjamin isn't *really* Frank Benjamin—he's Benjamin Franklin? *The* Benjamin Franklin?"

"Yes," Victor explained. "And he was kept alive inside this Leyden casket for over two hundred years."

"My crowning achievement!" declared Franklin. "After the glass armonica, of course."

Scott peered at the Leyden casket, a long metal and glass coffin that sat on a pedestal in the center of the laboratory. The look of awe on his face transformed into a wide grin. Above the casket hung a giant copper orb, suspended from the ceiling by heavy chains. Scott reached up to touch it.

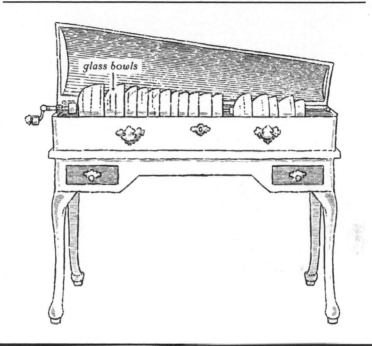

glass bowls

"Stop!" Victor yelled. "If you make contact, you'll fry your watch and your cell phone. The charging sphere works like a battery that collects and stores electrical energy. It will suck the power out of anything."

"Anything?" Scott asked.

"*Anything*. You can't just run around touching things, Scott. This laboratory is very dangerous."

"It's the greatest thing I've ever seen!"

"Splendid!" Franklin said, clapping his hands together. "I knew a true scientist such as yourself would appreciate this remarkable situation."

"But you can't tell anyone," Victor added. "There are still unanswered questions about why Ben was awakened."

"Victor is right," Franklin said. "As much as I would like to proclaim to the world who I truly am, I dare not. Revealing my identity might compromise our ability to respond to the Great Emergency."

"What's the Great Emergency?"

Franklin sighed. "Unfortunately, we do not yet know."

"But the voice on the other end of the electrophone might," Victor said. "It told us to check out news coverage of the bicycle parade."

"It's probably online already," Scott said. "My dad's station, WURP, is usually pretty quick about getting their stuff up on the Web."

Franklin and Scott peered over Victor's shoulders at the glowing computer screen.

"There it is," Scott said, pointing at the headline BICYCLE PARADE: RED, WHITE, AND AWESOME.

Victor clicked on the link and waited for the page to load. "What could this possibly have to do with the Modern Order of Prometheus?"

"That remains to be seen," Franklin said. "Let us keep a sharp eye."

A new page popped onto the screen, and Victor scanned

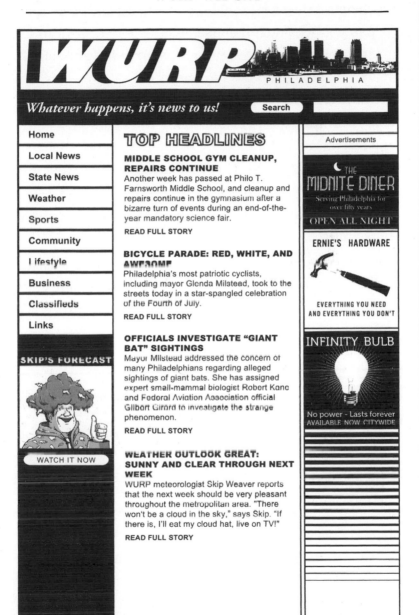

WURP
PHILADELPHIA

Whatever happens, it's news to us!   Search

| Home |
| Local News |
| State News |
| Weather |
| Sports |
| Community |
| Lifestyle |
| Business |
| Classifieds |
| Links |

SKIP'S FORECAST

WATCH IT NOW

TOP HEADLINES

MIDDLE SCHOOL GYM CLEANUP, REPAIRS CONTINUE
Another week has passed at Philo T. Farnsworth Middle School, and cleanup and repairs continue in the gymnasium after a bizarre turn of events during an end-of-the-year mandatory science fair.

READ FULL STORY

BICYCLE PARADE: RED, WHITE, AND AWESOME
Philadelphia's most patriotic cyclists, including mayor Glenda Milstead, took to the streets today in a star-spangled celebration of the Fourth of July.

READ FULL STORY

OFFICIALS INVESTIGATE "GIANT BAT" SIGHTINGS
Mayor Milstead addressed the concern of many Philadelphians regarding alleged sightings of giant bats. She has assigned expert small-mammal biologist Robert Kane and Federal Aviation Association official Gilbert Girard to investigate the strange phenomenon.

READ FULL STORY

WEATHER OUTLOOK GREAT: SUNNY AND CLEAR THROUGH NEXT WEEK
WURP meteorologist Skip Weaver reports that the next week should be very pleasant throughout the metropolitan area. "There won't be a cloud in the sky," says Skip. "If there is, I'll eat my cloud hat, live on TV!"

READ FULL STORY

it for any pertinent information. "It's just an article about the parade. Nothing too unusual."

Scott excitedly pointed at the screen. "What about that? That stuff about giant monster bats?"

"Monster bats?" Victor scoffed. "There's no such thing. Look here: it says that both the Federal Aviation Administration and a prominent small-mammal zoologist have studied the issue. These so-called bats are just illusions caused by swamp gas. Case closed."

"Swamp gas?" Scott said. "Do we even *have* swamps in Philadelphia?"

Victor rolled his eyes. "Please don't ask silly questions."

"Excuse me, boys," Franklin interrupted. "Can your computing machine allow us to see the lady mayor's press conference?"

Victor clicked on a picture of Mayor Milstead standing behind the microphone, and a video began to run. They watched the clip from beginning to end, listening carefully for clues.

"It's the same speech we heard when we were there," Victor said. "Nothing different."

Franklin rubbed his chin thoughtfully. "I've noticed two unusual things. First, as you remember, they spoke unusually slowly and deliberately. Why?"

"We already talked about that," Victor said. "They were nervous. I'd have a hard time speaking in front of a big crowd."

"Very well," Franklin said. "But I also found it peculiar that the gentleman from the Federal Aviation Administration said precisely the same thing as the man from the zoo. Word for word. You did notice this, didn't you, Victor?"

"Well, of—of course," Victor stammered. "How could anyone miss that?"

"Wouldn't you say that is a bit unusual?"

"You know what's unusual?" Scott said. "My grandma."

"I don't know if them using the same words is so strange," Victor said, ignoring Scott's comment. "They probably wrote the statement together."

"Hey," Scott said, "I just remembered something I noticed at the parade. Play it again."

Victor clicked on the picture.

"There!" Scott said. "I knew there was something weird about them. Zoom in on their eyes."

Victor moved the image of the mayor's head to the center of the screen and zoomed in. "Okay, that *is* weird."

"Her eyes," Franklin said. "Are they glowing?"

"It does look like it. Just a bit."

"Check out the other guys up there," Scott said.

Victor shifted the image around from Dr. Kane the zoologist to Mr. Girard of the FAA. Everyone's eyes had a faint red glow, except for the two men from the bike shop, who wore sunglasses.

"It could be a problem with the video encoding," Victor said.

"There's more," Franklin said gravely. "Look at the mayor's neck."

"Bite marks!" Scott gasped. "She was bitten. By the giant monster bats!"

Victor shook his head. "They're just moles, or birth-marks or—"

"Dr. Kane and Mr. Girard have them as well," Franklin said. "Does it seem likely that all three would have these marks in exactly the same places?"

"But the two men from the bike shop don't have any-thing on their necks."

"They wouldn't," Scott insisted.

"What do you mean?" Victor said.

"It all makes sense. Giant monster bats? People with bite marks on their necks talking all weird? Those guys from the bike shop *made* those bite marks. They aren't really bicycle repairmen at all—*they're vampires!*"

THAT NIGHT...

WURP investigative reporter Katie Kaitlyn reviewed her notes as she crossed the park on her way back to the sta-tion. There was no question about it. These giant bats were the real deal, and someone was trying to cover it up. But why?

She had seen one with her own eyes.

Two weeks ago, while walking to her car, she had glanced up. The ominous winged creature had been blacker than the night sky and so big that for one brief second, it blotted out the moon.

Swamp gas? Please. This story had conspiracy written all over it.

The latest interview was the icing on the cake. A high-ranking source in the police department had confirmed her suspicions.

Katie Kaitlyn wondered how far the cover-up went. The city council? The mayor?

She sat down on a bench beneath a streetlamp and phoned her producer. His voice mail picked up. No matter—she'd fill him in as soon as she got back to the station. If she hurried, the story would make the eleven o'clock news. It might even win her an award.

She stood up and put her phone and notes back into her purse.

The streetlamp flickered and then went out. She heard footsteps approaching, clacking on the pavement. Clutching her purse close, she rushed toward the corner.

As she hurried, the footsteps grew distant, but Katie Kaitlyn wasn't one to let her guard down. She began running faster. At her car door, she fumbled with her keys.

Fwoooooooooooooosh!

Something swooped in and bit her neck.

CHAPTER SIX
Franklinstein Unleashed!

Over the next few days, Franklin and Victor worked on improving the equipment in the basement laboratory. All the while, they monitored the electrophone for another message from the mysterious voice.

"This waiting," Franklin said, "it's driving me mad!"

"I understand," Victor said, "but the voice said you need to be here if we get another call. How's the temperature on the Hyperion coil?"

Franklin examined a gauge. "It is still running a trifle hot. Perhaps we should add more cooling agent."

On the floor in the corner, Scott was tinkering with his grandfather's broken radio. "What's a Hyperion coil?"

"My latest invention," Franklin explained. "Whenever

lightning strikes the house, the energy is stored inside the charging sphere." He pointed to the large copper orb suspended from the ceiling.

Scott walked over for a closer look.

"That generates a tremendous amount of heat," Victor continued. "When winter comes, we'll use some of it to heat the house. For now, the Hyperion coil fires the heat deep into the ground, where it dissipates in the cool earth. It's kind of like a super-powerful radiator."

"So that's why it's so hot in here," Scott said. "But I thought it was bad for lightning to hit your house."

Scott had endless questions, and there was plenty to tell: Franklin's invention of the life-sustaining harmonic fluid, his low-power zombie state, his overcharged

THE FRANKLIN HARMONIC COIL

charging sphere

thermostatic chamber

+ −

cooling agent

ground

harmonic coil

rampaging monster state, the battery belt that kept him in balance, and the real story behind the volcanic disaster at last month's Mandatory Science Fair.

"So all that stuff at the fair was because of you, Ben?" Scott asked.

"Well," Franklin said, "me, combined with your delectable potato battery exhibit."

"Yeah, those were awesome," Scott said, hefting his antique radio up on top of the Leyden casket. "Remember when you—"

"You really shouldn't put your radio there," Victor interrupted. "The casket's open."

"It's just for a second. I can't quite reach the thingamajig when it's on the floor." Scott turned, and bumped the radio with his elbow. It plunged into the harmonic fluid and sank to the bottom of the casket. The blue liquid bubbled and crackled.

"Don't worry," Scott said. "I'll get it."

"Young Master Weaver, perhaps you should step away from the casket," Franklin urged him. "It is not safe."

"Don't worry," Scott said, plunging his hands into the harmonic fluid. "The radio wasn't working anyway."

"Scott!" Victor yelled. "Don't!"

Scott fished around inside the casket. His hair stood straight up, and his eyes glowed turquoise. "It tingles!" He flashed an electric smile as he lifted out the soaking radio.

"Are you okay?" Victor asked.

"Sure," Scott said. "Maybe it even fixed the radio."

He flicked on the power switch and a horrible grating static blared from the speaker. The lights in the basement surged briefly.

"Nope, it's still broken," Scott said, over the static.

"Rrrrrrrrrrrrrrr!" Franklin growled.

Victor and Scott looked up from the radio. Their faces went pale.

"What's going on?" Scott said, slowly backing up.

"I don't know. It's like he's supercharged."

"But isn't that battery belt you invented supposed to keep him normal?"

Franklin lurched forward, his arms outstretched. He collided with a table, spilling beakers of cobalt and liquid franklinogen all over the floor. Victor tried to race out of the way but slipped, fell, and struck his head on a Leyden jar.

Scott clutched his radio and cowered behind the electrophone.

"Rrrrrrrrrrrrrrrrrgggghhhh!"

With one hand, Franklin flipped the electrophone on its side, smashing gauges and crushing pipes. He charged at Scott, madness in his eyes.

Victor blinked hard, trying to shake off the pain of his fall.

Franklin staggered closer to Scott, his clawlike fingers trembling with rage.

Wait a minute! Victor thought. "Scott! Turn off the radio!"

"But it's broken!"

"TURN IT OFF!"

Scott flicked the switch, and the radio fell silent. Franklin froze in place.

The old man looked startled. He scanned the room. "Good heavens, such a mess! What happened? Gentlemen, are you all right?"

The boys stared at Franklin.

"You don't remember, do you?" Victor asked.

"Of course I remember," Franklin said. "Young Master Weaver pulled his machine from the Leyden casket, he turned it on, and . . . and . . . what *did* happen?"

"After Scott turned on his radio, you went crazy—like you were supercharged."

"And when I turned off my radio," Scott continued, "you stopped going crazy."

Franklin reached for a stool. "Let me sit down and think this through." He clenched his eyes shut and rubbed his temples with his fingertips. "All I recall is that I had an unstoppable urge to tear the radio from your hands and smash it to pieces."

They all looked at Scott's radio. "Remarkable," Franklin said.

"See?" Scott said. "I told you it was broken."

CHAPTER SEVEN
Strangers at the Door

Victor and Scott did their best to straighten up the lab. Most of it could be easily repaired, but the electrophone was severely damaged. It would take considerable effort to get it working again.

As they cleaned up, Franklin sat slumped on a stool, recuperating.

"You don't look well," said Victor. "Maybe you should lie down."

Franklin mopped his brow with a handkerchief. "Perhaps just something to drink. And a morsel of food might be good. I'm still feeling a bit unsteady."

Victor and Scott helped Franklin up the ladder to his

apartment. They took special care to close the secret bookcase behind them.

"Victor," Franklin asked, "what is that smell?"

A tantalizing aroma drifted down from Victor's apartment. The three of them headed upstairs to investigate. Mrs. Godwin was in the kitchen, baking.

"Hey, Mom," said Victor. "That smells delicious. What is it?"

"It's for tomorrow's breakfast is what it is. Don't get any ideas."

"But—"

"No buts. You'll spoil your dinner." She opened the oven and pulled out a tray of blueberry muffins. "Oh, Mr. Benjamin! I didn't see you there."

"Good afternoon, Mrs. Godwin. I hope I'm not intruding."

Victor's mom smiled warmly at the old man. "Don't be silly. You know you're always welcome here. Please, sit down and have a muffin. You too, Scott. They're fresh from the oven."

Franklin winked at Victor. "*Eat to live, and not live to eat,* I always say. Except where muffins are concerned!"

"Thanks, Mrs. Godwin," said Scott. He sat down at the table next to Franklin and took a bite. "My mom makes muffins too. She says hers are healthy, but I like yours better."

"Thank you, Scott . . . I think." Mrs. Godwin handed a muffin to Victor. "So what are you boys up to?"

"Just working on some new projects," said Victor.

"Naturally." She shook her head. "Mr. Benjamin, I hope the boys aren't bothering you."

"Not in the least, Mrs. Godwin. In fact, Victor and Scott both have quite a talent for inventing. It is all I can do to keep up with them."

Mrs. Godwin pulled up a chair and sat down at the table. "So were you in the inventing business before you retired?"

"I dabbled," said Franklin. "I also worked with the public library, the post office, and the fire department. I was a printer for a while. I also worked in government."

"It sounds like a fascinating life," said Mrs. Godwin. "Can I get you another muffin?"

"I would be most obliged," said Franklin. "They are magnificent."

"You too, Scott?"

"Yes, please."

"Mom, can I—"

"You can have your second one for breakfast tomorrow." She took the plate of muffins to the counter and covered them. "Now I have some work to do in the study. While I'm in there, those muffins are off-limits. Understood?"

Victor sighed.

Mrs. Godwin walked down the hallway and closed a door behind her.

"Hey," Scott said, peering out the window, "it's those

guys from the parade—they're in your yard. See?"

Victor joined Scott at the window. The brothers from the Right Cycle Company were slinking around the yard, peeking in the downstairs windows, opening the mailbox, lifting up a flowerpot.

"It's like they're searching for something," Victor said. "But what? Let's get a closer look, Scott."

"A closer look? But—but they're vampires!"

"Victor has assured me that there are no such things as vampires," Franklin said. "Assuming this is true, I'd say further investigation is an excellent idea." He stood to join them.

"No, Ben," Victor insisted. "The voice from the electrophone told us that you need to stay out of sight. If those guys have some connection with the Great Emergency, we can't let them know that you've been awakened."

Franklin frowned. "I suppose you're right, Victor. I shall watch from up here. Do be careful."

Victor raced down the stairs, dragging Scott behind him.

They peered out the window beside the front door.

"We'll go about it scientifically," said Victor, trying not to sound afraid. "First, we have to gather data. Let's see if we can figure out what they're up to."

The brothers darted back and forth across the yard, picking up random objects, examining them briefly, and then dropping them. They pressed their ears against the ground, the car, and the walls of the house.

"Now it looks like they're listening for something," said Victor. "But what?"

"Vampires are bats, right?" said Scott. "And bats have super hearing. That's how they see!"

"Actually, bats have pretty good eyesight," said Victor. "And if these two *were* vampires, they wouldn't be running around in the middle of the day. In the movies, vampires vaporize in sunlight."

"That's why they're wearing hats and sunglasses. Hey, where are they?"

Victor looked out the window. "I think they're gone." He pulled the door open a crack.

The brothers were standing on the doorstep. He tried to slam the door . . .

Fwoooooooooosh!

. . . but somehow the brothers were already inside!

"Where is it?" the older brother growled.

"Wh-what?" Scott stammered.

"Where . . . is . . . it?" he repeated. The two men advanced toward the boys.

"I don't know what you mean." Victor's voice trembled. "Where's *what?*"

"The noise!" demanded the younger brother. *"What made the noise? It hurt! It hurt so much! We must . . ."*

". . . *DESTROY IT!*" the older brother finished, creeping closer.

Their ashen faces were now only inches away, their breath cold and musty. Victor squeezed his eyes shut. Scott guarded his neck with his hands.

The door at the top of the stairs swung open.

"Is everything all right?" Franklin boomed. He glared down at the brothers. "Gentlemen, it is time for you to take your leave."

The air crackled with static. Victor felt an electric shock run up his spine.

The two men reeled back, and Franklin's knees buckled. He stumbled down the stairs, clutching the banister for support. Scott rushed up to help.

The brothers staggered backward out the door and down the porch. Victor slammed the door shut and locked it. Through the window, he watched the two men teetering blindly down the street.

"Ben, are you okay?" said Victor.

Franklin shivered and slumped back against the stairs.

"What just happened?" asked Franklin.

"I'm not sure," said Victor, "but I have a bad feeling about those two."

"What two?" asked Franklin.

"The brothers from the bike shop," said Scott. "Don't you remember anything?"

"I remember some muffins. They were delicious."

"Let's get you back to your place," said Victor.

The two boys steadied the old man as he hobbled into

VAMPIRE IDENTIFICATION CHECKLIST

- ☐ Has very sharp fangs
- ☐ Drinks human blood
- ☐ Bites can turn normal people into vampires
- ☐ Possesses superhuman strength and speed
- ☐ Can hypnotize people with its eyes
- ☐ Pale complexion
- ☐ Must stay out of direct sunlight
- ☐ Can vanish into a mist, only to reappear elsewhere
- ☐ Cannot see its own reflection in a mirror

his apartment and settled onto the couch. They explained to him everything that had just happened.

"That was too close," said Victor. "If you hadn't come along when you did—"

"Yeah, what was that all about?" said Scott. "As soon as Ben showed up, it felt just like when I touch the electric fence at the zoo. I forget, does electricity repel vampires?"

"They're *not* vampires," said Victor. "But I have to admit, there is something very strange about them."

Franklin held his hands in front of him, wiggling his fingers as if to make sure they still worked. "Why do you suppose they came here? What were they looking for?"

"Some kind of sound," said Victor. "They wanted to destroy it. But we didn't make any sound."

"I did, remember?"

Victor and Franklin turned to Scott.

"I mean, I was just thinking," said Scott, "when my grandfather's radio made that noise, Ben tried to destroy it. Maybe *they* heard it too."

Victor shook his head. "I don't think so. When the radio fell into the harmonic fluid, it must have been changed somehow. Ben is affected by the radio because of his unique biology. He's powered by harmonic fluid."

"Unless," said Franklin, "my biology is not so unique."

"What do you mean?"

"Perhaps the brothers are also powered by harmonic fluid. That might explain the strange reaction in the stairway."

Scott scratched his head. "But I thought only people in the Modern Order of Prometheus had that stuff inside them."

"So did I," said Franklin. "I think it's our turn to pay the brothers a visit."

CHAPTER EIGHT
The Right Cycle Company

The next morning, Victor, Scott, and Franklin set off for the bike shop. Scott pedaled ahead as Franklin struggled to remain upright on his bike. The oversized training wheels Victor had installed on both front and back axles were the only things keeping him anywhere close to vertical. Was it possible he was actually getting *worse* with practice?

Yet Franklin refused to give up—he was determined to conquer what he called "the devil's contraption." Victor brought up the rear, walking and pushing his own mangled bike.

"It is unfortunate that you crashed your bicycle in your rush to reach the electrophone," Franklin said, "but you must admit, it provides a perfect excuse for visiting the repair shop."

At the corner, Victor called for Scott to wait while he checked his map. The bike shop was close, and he wanted to get his bearings before they arrived.

"Look, there's my dad," said Scott. He waved his arms. "Dad! Over here!"

Victor groaned. Across the street, an enormous foam bicycle seat was handing out pamphlets to passersby. The seat had arms, legs, and Skip Weaver's face smack-dab in the middle, where a giant biker's butt would sit. *This* was WURP's chief meteorologist?

"Hey, buddy!" said the seat. "How's it going?"

"We don't have time for this," Victor whispered to Ben. "We're on a mission."

"Mister Weaver!" Franklin called. "Good morning to you!"

Franklin and Scott wheeled their bikes across the street. Reluctantly, Victor followed.

"Dad, you remember my friends Victor and Mr. Frank— er, Mr. *Benjamin*? Mr. Frank Benjamin?"

"Sure do," said Skip, handing each of them a pamphlet. "How are you fellas doing today? Interested in a free tune- up for those bikes? Special deal, one day only."

"As a matter of fact, we are," said Victor. "Are you work- ing for the Right Cycle Company?"

"Just some temporary promo work to help the guys get the business off the ground. Standard celebrity stuff."

Victor couldn't help thinking that dressed as a giant seat, Skip Weaver didn't look much like a celebrity.

"Also, the station's making me pay them back for the camera I broke a few days ago."

"I remember—when you made the sun chase the clouds away!" Franklin chuckled. "That was most entertaining."

"Then it was all worth it!"

"Tell me, Mr. Weaver," asked Franklin. "Are cameras expensive?"

Skip Weaver's smile disappeared. "You have no idea." He slumped down onto a step, but his foam rubber suit bounced him back up.

"Stupid costume!" Skip complained. "I can't even sit down."

There was an awkward silence. Finally, Victor said, "Well, we really should be going now."

"Of course," Skip said. "Enjoy your day, boys. Nice seeing you again, Mr. Benjamin."

Around the corner, Victor paused.

"The bike shop is on the next block. It's unlikely the brothers remember any more about their visit to our house than you do, Ben. Just the same, we'd better play it safe. Scott, do you have the disguises?"

"Right here." He pulled two wigs from a brown paper bag and held them up for inspection. "Do you want long hair or curly?"

"I'll take curly." Victor carefully pulled the wig over his

own hair. "Technically, it's the most dissimilar to my own hair. Plus, since I'm wearing my old glasses, it will—hey, what's so funny?"

"Nothing, my boy," said Franklin, struggling to maintain his composure. "You look fine, just like . . . like . . ."

"Like an old lady!" finished Scott. At that, both he and Franklin burst into howls of laughter.

"Very funny," said Victor dryly. "All right, Scott. Let's see what *you* look like."

Scott pulled his wig over his head, and Franklin stopped laughing almost immediately.

"Oh, my. Scott, that does make you look distinguished. Bravo."

"Whatever," grumbled Victor. "Ben, remember to keep your distance from the brothers."

"I'll wait for you across the street," Franklin said. "Be careful, boys."

It was easy to spot the Right Cycle Company. Dozens of customers with bikes snaked out the door and down the block. Victor and Scott joined the back of the line.

"I don't get it," said Scott. "How are they going to make any money fixing all these bikes for free? It'll take them forever."

"I was wondering the same thing," said Victor. "It doesn't add up."

IS PLEASED TO OFFER

to the citizens of the great city of

PHILADELPHIA

 # FREE

BICYCLE REPAIR

AND "TUNE-UP"

SATURDAY, JULY 7

All Day

ALL MANNER OF BICYCLES WELCOME

The line moved much more quickly than they expected, and before long, they were inside. Aside from all the people, the store was strangely empty. There were no helmets, bike pumps, or even bicycles for sale. Only a long counter at the back, behind which the brothers rapidly checked in customers.

Something was wrong. The brothers weren't just fast, they were *too* fast, moving with the precision of robots. The younger brother handled the paperwork, filling out forms with his left hand while simultaneously sorting and filing with his right. Meanwhile, the older brother collected the bikes and wheeled them through a door to a room in the back. Victor did a quick estimate. In just one morning, they would easily take in hundreds, maybe a thousand bikes. But why?

Victor adjusted his wig and tried to look manly. At home, the disguises had seemed like a good idea. But now, so close to the brothers, it all just felt foolish. These men were dangerous.

"Next!"

The sound of the younger brother's voice snapped Victor back to reality. He stepped forward and handed over his bike.

"Name?"

Victor froze. Why hadn't he thought to prepare a fake name? Of course they would ask. "John," he sputtered. "John, uh . . . uh . . ."

"Johnson!" added Scott.

"Telephone number?"

Automatically, Victor rattled off the digits of his cell phone number. By the time he realized his mistake, the brother had moved on to the next customer.

Outside, the boys paused to discuss what had just happened.

"Why'd you give them your real phone number?" asked Scott. "Do you want them to call us?"

Victor winced. "Of course not. I just . . . I panicked."

"That's okay. I don't think they recognized us."

"If they did, they hid it well," Victor agreed. "Where do you think they're taking all the bikes?"

"Let's find out." Scott disappeared around the corner, down an alley. Victor trailed behind. He was surprised to see that the small Right Cycle Company storefront was connected to an enormous warehouse at the back.

"Wow," said Victor. "They could put a million bikes in there if they wanted to."

"Help me with these garbage cans," said Scott. He dragged one under a high window. "I want to look inside."

"I don't know . . ."

"Trust me," said Scott. Together, he and Victor lifted another garbage can onto the stack and balanced it between two others. "I climb up stuff all the time. This will work."

It did work, although Victor wasn't entirely sure how. Like most of Scott's projects, this one had all the signs of an impending disaster. Scott climbed up first, and reluctantly, Victor followed. Side by side, they balanced on their toes and held tight to the windowsill. Scott's tower wobbled, but it held.

"I don't believe it," whispered Victor, peering through the dusty window. "There *are* a million bikes in there."

Inside, the door banged open. Scott and Victor ducked as the older brother wheeled another bicycle into the room. They watched him grip it tightly and tear the wheels off with his bare hands. He threw the tires onto one heaping pile, the handlebars onto another, then effortlessly flung the bicycle frame on top of a third. It bounced off the high ceiling and tumbled down the side. The whole process took less than ten seconds.

"He's *strong*," whispered Scott. "And not very nice to those bikes."

The brother tipped his head, then suddenly spun toward the window. He stared directly at Scott and Victor, his eyes glowing red.

"He sees us!" said Victor.

Scott leapt to the ground. Victor tried to climb down, but slipped. The tower of garbage cans collapsed around him, crashing to the pavement. The boys took off down the alley.

Across the street, they found Franklin waiting with the bikes, pretending to read a newspaper.

"We have to"—Victor huffed—"we have to get out of here, now!"

Franklin lowered the newspaper. "Haste makes waste, Victor. What's happened?"

Victor pointed back across the street.

The brother stood at the entrance to the alley, squinting in the sunlight. "It is *YOU*!" he roared, shielding his eyes from the light. *"Benjamin Franklin!"*

The brother started toward them just as the traffic light changed. Cars sped down the street, and he jumped back onto the curb, furious.

"Forget what I said," shouted Franklin. "Make haste! *Flee!*"

OTHER FRANKLIN APHORISMS

Early to bed and early to rise, makes
a man healthy, wealthy, and wise.

No gains without pains.

Fish and visitors stink in three days.

Eat to live, and not live to eat.

Men and melons are hard to know.

CHAPTER NINE
Piecing It Together

"Did we lose him?" Victor wheezed, glancing back. He ran alongside Franklin, guiding the old man's handlebars to keep him upright.

"I don't know," Scott said. "Follow me. I know a place!"

He led them off the road into an alley. A chain-link fence blocked the exit. Scott skidded to a halt, jumped off his bike, and pulled up a patch of fence. "This way!"

After Franklin and Victor wedged through, Scott pulled their bikes under.

Victor looked around. "What *is* this place?"

"It's the Arthur Parker Art Park. My mom takes me here sometimes. She's on the board."

"How come I've never heard of it before?" Victor said.

"It's private," Scott explained. "This is where rich people keep their outdoor art when they don't have enough room for it in their yards."

"I am confused," Franklin said. "Where exactly is the art?"

"Everywhere," Scott said. "This place is gigantic."

He pointed across the field to a concrete cupcake the size of an automobile. Fifty yards beyond, a giant pair of stainless-steel tube socks wrestled on a taco shell. Franklin walked over to something that looked like a colossal roll of toilet paper.

"Royal Flush," Franklin read off a plaque. "Art certainly has changed since my day."

They collapsed onto the grass, hiding behind an enormous penny, and waited to see if anyone had followed them. The park was deserted. Once they decided they were in the clear, Victor and Scott filled Franklin in on what they had seen at the bicycle shop.

"Interesting," Franklin said. "But what to make of it all?"

"Let's look at this systematically," Victor said. "What do we know for sure?"

"We know the brothers run a bicycle repair shop."

"But they tear the bikes apart instead of fixing them," Scott added.

"They have a strange connection with me," Franklin continued. "And they know who I am. What else?"

Victor remembered the bicycle parade. "They also have

some sort of connection with Mayor Milstead, Mr. Girard, and Dr. Kane."

"And they're probably vampires," Scott said. "Remember the bite marks?"

Victor shook his head. "Scott, there are no such things as vampires."

"Are we forgetting anything else?" Franklin asked.

Scott began to laugh. "I just thought of something. Those bicycle guys are brothers, right? And they work at the Right Cycle Company? That makes them 'the Right brothers'! You know, like the inventors, the Wright brothers."

"The Wright brothers?" Franklin asked. "Who are they?"

"Back in the early nineteen hundreds, two brothers named Orville and Wilbur Wright invented the airplane," Victor explained. "An amazing achievement, considering that they started out as . . ."

Victor paused.

"They started out as what?" Franklin asked.

"Bicycle repairmen!" He smacked his hand on his forehead. "Of course! Those aren't the Right brothers. They're the *WRIGHT* brothers!"

"Hold on," Scott said. "If they invented the airplane in the early nineteen hundreds, wouldn't that make them over a hundred years old?"

"So?" Victor nodded toward Franklin. "Ben's at least three hundred years old. Which must mean—"

"That they're members of the Modern Order of Pro-

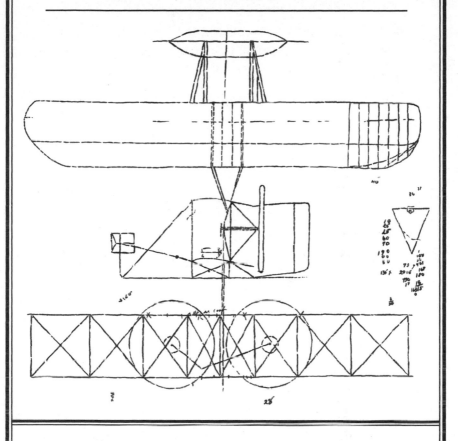

metheus!" Franklin said. "If these brothers did invent the airplane, they must have been remarkable men. It makes sense that the Order would have preserved them before they died."

"That would explain why they were drawn to Scott's harmonically charged radio," Victor said, "just like you were."

"But how come they're acting like bad guys?" Scott asked. "You should have seen them ripping those bikes apart. That's not what the Order is supposed to be about, is it?"

"No, it is not," agreed Franklin.

"Plus, they're vampires. You're not a vampire, are you?"

"They are *not vampires*!" Victor snapped.

"Whatever they are, we need answers." Franklin scratched his chin. "Our best strategy is to repair the damage I did to the electrophone. We must return to the laboratory at once!"

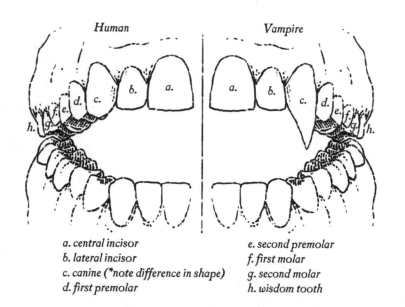

A COMPARISON OF HUMAN AND VAMPIRE TEETH

a. central incisor
b. lateral incisor
c. canine (*note difference in shape)
d. first premolar
e. second premolar
f. first molar
g. second molar
h. wisdom tooth

CHAPTER TEN
A Close Cull

Before they could fix the electrophone, they needed new parts. That meant a visit to Ernie's hardware store.

Victor loved his cousin's store. Sure, it was dark, musty, and completely disorganized. But if you were looking for just the right part to make your project work—and were willing to do a little digging—you could find it at Ernie's.

Franklin, Scott, and Victor found Ernie behind the counter, thumbing through an old copy of *Popular Quantum Mechanics*.

"Hey, cousin!" Ernie said. "What's goin' on, electron?"

Victor smiled. "Hi, Ernie. You remember Mr. Benjamin, right? And this is my friend Scott."

"Salutations, brothers," Ernie said.

Ernie sported a ten-gallon cowboy hat. Dozens of loops were sewn around its hatband; they held pens, pencils, fingernail clippers, screwdrivers, a jeweler's hammer, a small flashlight, and, of course, Tootsie Rolls.

He popped one into his mouth and tossed one each to Victor, Scott, and Franklin. "So, Victor, what can I do ya for?"

"We're working on a project and need a few things. Some freon metacoiling, an Ehlinger switch, a couple of strontium diodes—"

"I'll tell you what," Ernie interrupted. "I was just about to step out and grab a bite. Would you guys mind watching the shop? Dig up whatever junk you're looking for, throw it in a bag, and I'll ring you up when I get back."

After about a half hour, they had found everything they needed. Victor and Franklin put it all in a bag. As they waited for Ernie to return, Scott played with a stapler he found behind the counter. "Staplers are cool."

"I couldn't agree more," Franklin said. "Throw it in the bag."

Victor's cell phone rang.

"That's odd," he said. "Usually the caller's name and number appear on the screen." He pressed a button. "Hello?"

It was a man's voice. *"I must speak with Dr. Franklin."*

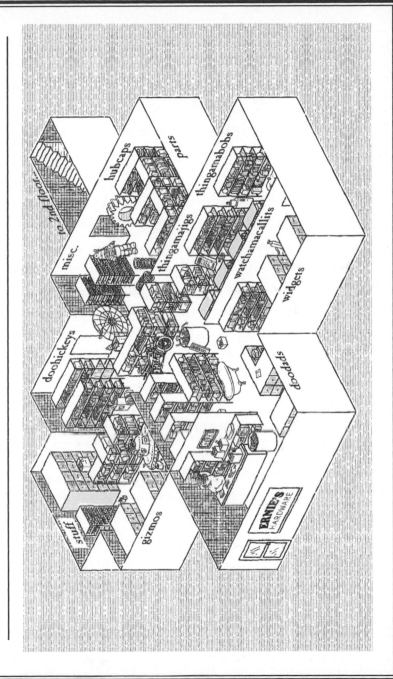

Floor plan of Ernie's Hardware Store

"What?" Victor was stunned. "How do you know—who is this?"

"I must speak with Dr. Benjamin Franklin immediately," the voice insisted. *"This is the Modern Order of Prometheus!"*

Victor stared at the phone for a moment, then handed it to Franklin. "It's for you. He says he's from the Order."

"The Order!" Franklin gasped. "Is it the same voice from the electrophone?"

Victor shook his head. "I don't think so. This guy has an accent."

Franklin took the phone and held it to his ear. "Hello? This is Dr. Franklin. Who is speaking?"

A piercing siren blasted from the phone. Franklin's face suddenly went blank. He stood stock-still.

"His eyes!" Scott said, pointing at Franklin. "They're changing color."

Red!

"Come on!" Victor dragged Scott down an aisle toward the back of the store.

They peered through a shelf. Franklin flung the phone into the air. He pressed his hands against his ears and roared.

"He's acting the same way he did when my radio got wet!" Scott said.

"It must be the phone," Victor said. "We've got to shut it off!"

Franklin snapped his head at the sound of Victor's

voice. He thrust his arms toward the boys, fingers clutching the air, and charged down the aisle.

"Or we could just get out of here!" Scott said, running for the exit.

SMASH!

A bathtub sailed over their heads, crashed onto the floor, and slid to a stop, blocking the door. The boys whirled around to see Franklin searching for something else heavy to throw.

"Rrrrrrrrraaarrrrrrrggghhhhh!"

Victor and Scott fled down another twisting aisle.

You could get lost in this place, Victor thought. *Good thing!*

At the end of the next aisle, Scott scrambled up a tall shelf stacked high with hubcaps.

"Where are you going?" Victor whispered.

"Up!"

Victor struggled to the top. They lay flat on their stomachs, inches from the ceiling, and listened to Franklin's heavy footsteps below them. Victor tried hard not to breathe.

"That noise is making him crazy," Victor whispered. "Did you see where he threw the phone?"

"I can hear it, but I can't see it," Scott whispered. "Uh-oh."

"What?"

"Dust. I'm . . . allergic. . . . *Aaaaa-choo!*"

Franklin's head jerked up. He swung his arm and struck the shelf, tipping it over. Victor, Scott, and hundreds of hubcaps crashed onto the hard floor below. The clatter enraged Franklin.

Victor froze.

Scott sprang to his feet. He picked up one of the hubcaps, aimed, and flung it Frisbee-style. It flew through the air, past Franklin's head, and crashed against the ceiling.

Franklin swatted at the air. He roared and shook his fists.

"Cut it out!" Victor said. "You're just making him angrier!"

Scott grabbed another hubcap and hurled it. Again, it narrowly missed Franklin and bounced off the ceiling.

Franklin's eyes burned brighter. He clambered over the fallen shelf toward the boys.

"Even if you hit him, it's not going to do any good," Victor insisted. "He's too powerful!"

"I'm not aiming at *him*."

Scott picked up a third hubcap, squinted into the distance, and flung it. The hubcap whizzed over Franklin's head and ricocheted off a broken ceiling fan. A small object fell from one of the fan's blades.

Victor's phone!

"I'll distract him!" Scott said. "Get to your phone and turn it off!"

Scott grabbed another hubcap, aimed, and hurled it at

Franklin. It bounced off his forehead. Franklin shook his head, and Scott flung another. Then another.

Victor scrambled around the rubble, dove for the phone, and pushed the Off button. The noise ceased.

Franklin froze. His eyes slowly softened back to their natural blue.

Scott ran to Victor's side. "You okay?"

"Thanks to you," Victor said. "That was genius."

Franklin blinked. He looked confused. "Weren't we just . . . somewhere else?"

They tried their best to clean up Cousin Ernie's store, but it was impossible. Franklin had done too much damage.

"Am I to understand," Franklin said, "that I took a phone call from someone claiming to be from the Modern Order of Prometheus, my eyes went red, and I came at you?"

"You threw a bathtub," said Scott.

"Heavens! I shall never answer a telephone again. It seems Victor and I owe you a debt of gratitude, Scott."

"We have to get to the bottom of this, before someone gets hurt," Victor said. "Ben, did you recognize that voice? Do you remember anything at all?"

"Only rage . . . confusion . . . It felt as if someone other than I was controlling my actions."

A bell rang and the front door opened. Ernie walked in, holding half a cheesecake in his hand.

"Hey, guys. Thanks for watching the place." He stopped and looked around the room, stunned. "What happened here?"

"Ernie, I can explain everything," Victor began. "You see, we had a minor—"

"It looks fantastic!" Ernie said, a broad smile on his face. "Thanks for tidying up. No charge for the stuff."

OTHER USES FOR A BATHTUB BESIDES THROWING IT

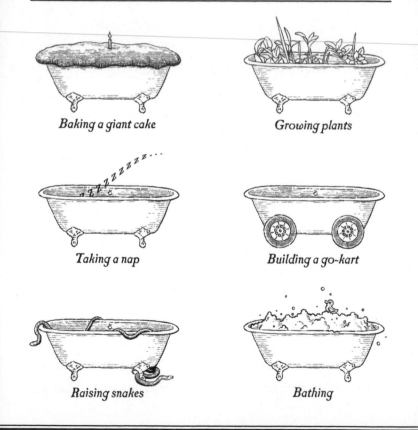

Baking a giant cake

Growing plants

Taking a nap

Building a go-kart

Raising snakes

Bathing

Benjamin Franklinstein Meets the Fright Brothers

CHAPTER ELEVEN
A Mysterious Message

By the time they got back to Victor's house, it was late afternoon and they were exhausted. Franklin needed to recharge his battery belt, so they agreed to meet after dinner in the basement laboratory. Scott biked home to ask his parents if he could sleep over at Victor's.

Around seven o'clock Victor grabbed the equipment he had collected at Ernie's and headed downstairs to Franklin's apartment. He pulled open the secret bookcase, lowered the bag of parts down the shaft with a rope, then climbed down the ladder. Franklin was busy at the workbench poring over a book on the history of famous inventors. It was open to a chapter on the Wright brothers.

"Look at this photograph!" Franklin mused. "Can you

imagine the thrill the first time their invention actually took flight? They must have felt like gods."

Franklin handed the book to Victor. The men in the picture were younger, but there was no mistaking their similarity to the brothers in the bicycle shop.

"Such a fantastic machine!" Franklin continued. "It saddens me to think that they may be using their genius to do the world harm."

"I know," said Victor. He emptied the bag of parts onto the workbench and began to sort through them. "But I can't help feeling there's more to the story. If we can just get the electrophone fixed, maybe the mysterious voice at the other end can help us figure it out."

"But can we trust the voice on the electrophone?" Franklin asked. "After what happened to me at Ernie's—"

"No, the voice on the cell phone was different, I'm sure of it," Victor said. "The voice on the electrophone is on our side. Plus, I'll be here to turn it off if anything goes wrong."

For the next hour, Victor and Franklin worked on the electrophone. Scott arrived with his backpack and sleeping bag as they were finishing up.

"Sorry I'm late. My dad came home and tried to squeeze through the front door wearing his bicycle seat costume. We spent an hour pulling him free. He says hi."

"You're just in time," said Victor. "I think we've got the electrophone fixed, and we're about to turn it on."

"Do you think it's safe?" Scott asked. "The bad guys might still be listening in."

"I fear we have no other choice," Franklin said. "The urgency of our situation demands we try."

"We'll keep it short," Victor agreed. "Ben, I think you should speak this time. The voice specifically asked for you." He opened the broadcast valves and cranked the charging wheel. Franklin picked up the copper speaking cone and held it in front of his mouth.

"This is Dr. Franklin," he announced. "We need to speak to you urgently about the Wright brothers. Are you there? I repeat: are you there?"

The speaker bubbled and crackled. For several minutes, they listened to the empty static. Finally, a faint voice said, *"Mérida, Mexico."*

The three looked at one another. Mexico?

"I'm not sure I understand," Franklin said into the cone. "You want us to meet you in Mexico? That will not be possible. Please clarify."

"Niort, France."

"Scott," Victor whispered, "hand me that pen and paper."

"I'm afraid we cannot meet you in France, either," continued Franklin. "Perhaps—"

"Edinburgh, Scotland . . . Neryungri, Russia . . . Five Finger, Alaska . . . Nejran, Saudi Arabia."

Victor scribbled furiously. The voice repeated the entire list once more, and then the electrophone went silent.

★ ★ ★

Half an hour later Victor, Scott, and Franklin were enjoying a snack in the Godwin kitchen, huddled around a large map of the world. Mrs. Godwin was in the living room watching TV.

"There's Five Finger, Alaska," said Scott, pointing at the map. "Maybe we're supposed to go there."

Victor shook his head. "I don't think that's what this is about. The last time we spoke, the voice said that someone might be listening in. What if these locations are actually some sort of coded message?"

"I was thinking the same thing," Franklin said. "When General Washington commanded the Continental Army, his coded messages helped us win the war. Let us find the other locations on the map."

"Here's Edinburgh," said Victor, circling it in red. "And Neryungri, Russia. There's Saudi Arabia . . ."

"I see Niort," said Scott.

"There's Nejran," said Franklin. "And there, near the tip of Mexico, I see Mérida. But what does it all mean?"

Even with all the cities plotted on the map, the message wasn't any clearer. There didn't seem to be any logical order to the locations. Victor tried rearranging the letters in their names. Franklin suggested connecting the cities with lines, with the thought that they might form some sort of shape, like an arrow. Scott wanted to buy tickets and fly to each city.

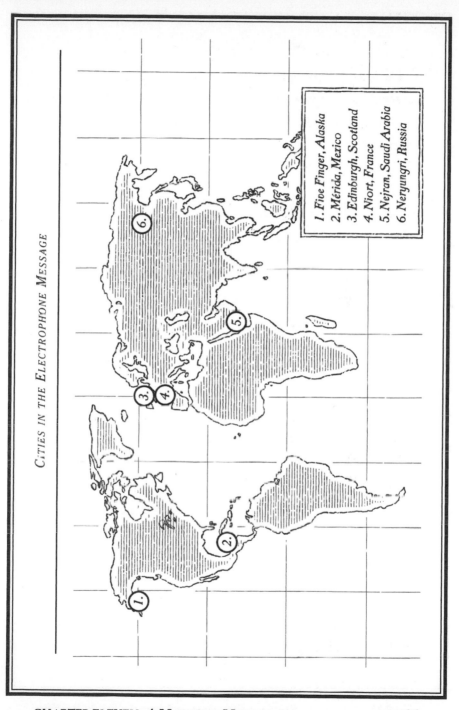

1. Five Finger, Alaska
2. Mérida, Mexico
3. Edinburgh, Scotland
4. Niort, France
5. Nejran, Saudi Arabia
6. Neryungri, Russia

After several hours of frustration, they called it quits. Franklin wished everyone a good night and agreed to meet the next morning to try again. Victor and Scott joined Mrs. Godwin in the living room and collapsed onto the couch, exhausted.

"Did you boys get anywhere with your puzzle?" she asked.

"Not really," said Scott. "It's a tough one."

"I'm sure you'll figure it out." She turned off the TV. "I heard you mention Edinburgh. I was there years ago."

Victor perked up. "You were?"

"Only for a short time. It was an emergency stopover on the way to Paris."

"What happened?"

"There was a terrible storm. Lightning struck the wing, and we lost an engine. We weren't sure we were going to make it." She shuddered. "I was never so happy to see an airport in my entire life."

"Wow. You don't remember anything special about Edinburgh, do you?"

She shook her head. "Only the terminal. We spent a couple of hours there waiting for them to put us on a new flight."

Victor sighed, disappointed at hitting yet another dead end.

"Hey, Mrs. Godwin, have you ever been to Nejran?" Scott asked. "Or Niort? Or Five Finger, Alaska; Mérida,

Mexico; or Neryungri, Russia?"

Mrs. Godwin laughed. "I've never even heard of those places." She looked at her watch. "Speaking of trips, isn't it time you two took a trip up to bed?"

Victor struggled to fall asleep. Every muscle in his body was exhausted, but his mind was racing. Something in his mother's story nagged at him. The airplane? The storm? The airport?

When he finally did fall asleep, he had terrible dreams. At one point he, Scott, and Franklin were flying in a fierce storm. Their plane rocked from side to side as lightning flashed in the sky. Through the window, Victor could see the Wright brothers flying closer and closer in their old-fashioned airplane. Their fangs were long and sharp, and their eyes glowed bright red.

Then Victor was in an airport. Franklin, Scott, and the Wright brothers were gone. He stood alone in front of an enormous departure board, frantically searching for a flight home. He looked down the list of destinations but couldn't make out the names of the cities. They were scrambled, as if in some sort of code.

Code.

Airport code.

In a flash, Victor was wide awake, his heart pounding. It was four A.M. He raced to his computer and began entering the names of the cities from the list.

As he suspected, each city was home to an airport. Each airport, Victor knew, had its own three-letter international code, used by pilots and air traffic controllers to identify them easily.

Victor grabbed a piece of paper. Scanning the list on the computer screen, he scribbled down the airport codes for each of the cities.

Mérida, Mexico: MID
Niort, France: NIT
Edinburgh, Scotland: EDI
Neryungri, Russia: NER
Five Finger, Alaska: FIV
Nejran, Saudi Arabia: EAM

He knew exactly what the mysterious voice had been trying to tell them.

There was no time to waste. He woke up Scott.

MEANWHILE . . .

It was four A.M. Police Chief Elmore Hawkins gazed at the sliver of moon high above his city. Confusion swirled in his head. Days had passed since Mayor Milstead and her experts had determined that the giant flying bats were only swamp gas mirages. But he was certain he had caught a glimpse of something only a week before, and it had looked real enough to him.

He had poked around City Hall, asking questions, trying to get his hands on the official report, but no luck. The word from above was that it had been settled. Swamp gas.

But that wasn't good enough. In the morning he would open his own investigation. Sure, he'd take some heat from the mayor, but he was respected in the community and could weather the political storm.

He turned a corner and walked past a thin, mustached man dressed all in black. An odd-looking man, the chief thought. Something about his eyes . . . They almost seemed to glow in the lamplight.

"Hi," Chief Hawkins said.

The man nodded.

The chief walked past him, then felt a sharp bite on his neck.

He slapped at it, thinking a bug had bitten him. When he looked at his palm, he noticed two small splotches of blood.

Fwoooooooosh!

He spun around. Hadn't there been a man standing there? Everything was going fuzzy. What had he been thinking about before he was bitten? He suddenly couldn't remember.

He couldn't remember . . . anything. But he knew where he had to go.

CHAPTER TWELVE
Breakfast at the Midnite Diner

It was four fifty in the morning when Victor, Scott, and Franklin arrived at the Midnite Diner. Although the rest of the street was still asleep, the Midnite was alive with the aroma of breakfast cooking on the griddle and the sounds of lively conversation.

"It smells delicious," marveled Franklin. "And it's only a few blocks from our house! Why have we never eaten here before?"

At the counter sat a biker, a musician with green hair, and an elderly woman with thick glasses and a poodle in her purse. The booths were filled with similarly colorful characters, all chatting in various languages.

"I don't know," said Victor. "I guess I've always been a little afraid of this place."

"Afraid?" said Franklin. "Victor, how many times must I tell you, science—and fine dining—is risk! Really, you should get out more."

"There's nothing to be scared of," added Scott, leading them toward an empty booth in the back. "This place is great."

"You've been here before?"

"All the time. My dad's a regular." He nodded toward the wall.

Hanging above the table was an enormous framed, autographed photo of Skip Weaver, weatherman. For some reason, he was in his underpants. Victor shook his head. In a place like the Midnite Diner, Scott's dad would fit right in.

"So why are we here, anyway?" Scott asked. "And why so early?"

"We're here to meet the voice from the electrophone," said Victor. He scanned the room. "Keep your eyes peeled. It could be anyone, and he might be in disguise."

"But how do you know?" Franklin asked. "You still haven't explained how you deciphered the message."

"There was no time. We had to get here right away." Victor set the piece of paper with his notes on the table. "It finally hit me: this is all about the Wright brothers and airplanes. Each one of the cities on the list has an airport, and each airport has a three-letter code."

Franklin studied the page. "I see! Well done, Victor."

"I don't get it," said Scott.

"Put the city codes in a row, one after the other," Victor explained. "Like this: MID, NIT, EDI, NER, FIV, EAM. Then change the spaces: MIDNITE DINER FIVE AM."

"Cool!"

"We're still early," said Franklin. "Shall we order some pancakes?"

OTHER AIRPORT CODES OF NOTE

Atmautluak, Alaska	ATT
Enewetak Atoll, Marshall Islands	ENT
Impfondo, Congo	ION
Columbus, New Mexico	CUS
Tioman, Malaysia	TOD
Kiana, Alaska	IAN
Strathmore, Australia	STH
El Encanto, Colombia	ECO
Sangley Point, Philippines	NSP
Kirakira, Solomon Islands	IRA
Corryong, Australia	CYG
Roswell, New Mexico	ROW
Stutgart, Germany	STR
St. Augustine, Florida	UST
Nosara Beach, Costa Rica	NOB
Oudomxay, Laos	ODY

Benjamin Franklinstein Meets the Fright Brothers

Five o'clock, then five thirty came and went, with no contact from the mysterious voice. Franklin and Scott ordered more pancakes. Victor was too edgy to eat.

"I wonder if we're doing this wrong," he said. "Maybe we're supposed to get up and introduce ourselves."

"To who?" asked Scott.

Victor shrugged. "I don't know. Maybe the cook. We could tell him we're here to meet someone."

"Good luck!" Scott laughed. "He doesn't speak English, except for the stuff on the menu."

"Do you recognize anyone else?" asked Franklin.

"Not really," said Scott. "I'm not usually here this early. It's a different crowd."

"Maybe we should just—"

"Shove over," said a voice. "Act like you know me."

Victor looked up. Standing above him was a tall, thin girl about his age, dressed entirely in black. She wore a hooded sweatshirt and peered at them over a pair of dark sunglasses.

"Are you deaf? I said move over."

Victor slid to his left, and the girl sat down next to him.

"He may be watching us, so we don't have a lot of time. Dr. Franklin, it's an honor to meet you. I'm Jaime Winters."

Franklin held out his hand. "The honor is mine, young lady. Are you, by chance, a Custodian?"

"My parents are . . . I mean, were," said Jaime. "And

it's probably best if we don't say that word too loudly. He might be listening."

"Who might be listening?" Scott asked.

Jaime glared at him. "Who are you, exactly?"

"My name's Scott." He pointed at the picture above him. "That's my dad."

"Look," said Jaime, "I don't think you boys understand what's going on here, so I'll try to make it as simple as possible. I have business with Dr. Franklin, and it's not really kid stuff. Maybe it's best if you just run along."

Victor bristled. "And how old are *you*?"

"I assure you, Miss Winters," offered Franklin, "these gentlemen have my complete confidence."

Jaime looked at Victor and Scott with contempt. "As you wish, Dr. Franklin."

"Please, call me Ben."

"All right, Ben." Her voice dropped to a whisper. "Something bad is going down, and we don't have much time. The Modern Order of Prometheus is in trouble, and Custodians are disappearing. We suspect that a few of them, like your own Custodian, Mr. Mercer, may have been murdered."

"Mr. Mercer was our downstairs neighbor," said Victor. "He wasn't murdered. He died of a heart attack."

Jaime rolled her eyes. "Did you do an autopsy? I didn't think so. Now, listen carefully. There are only a few of us left, and every time we speak on the electrophone or go out in public, we put ourselves at risk. I'm in great danger right now. Don't make me repeat myself."

"Sorry," said Victor.

"You guys figured out the Wright brothers have been awakened. That confirms our suspicions. Their Custodian stopped responding to our messages several weeks ago."

"Forgive me," said Franklin, "but when you say 'our' messages, do you mean you and your parents?"

"My parents disappeared months ago," said Jaime. She paused and took a deep breath. "Now it's just me and a handful of other Custodians from the Order. We call ourselves the Promethean Underground."

"P-U!" said Scott. "That's funny!"

Jaime scowled. "We've been working in secret, gathering whatever information we can. This latest business with the Wright brothers has us very concerned."

"Why?" asked Franklin. "What are they planning?"

"We have no idea, and that's why we need your help. We do know that the brothers appear to be under the control of someone calling himself the Emperor. We believe he's done something to their Custodian."

"You said my own Custodian was killed," said Franklin. "Did this Emperor awaken me for the same reason he awakened the Wright brothers?"

"We believe so."

"Then why am I not under his control as well?"

"We don't know. For some reason, you were immune.

After he failed with you, he tried again, this time with the brothers."

"Wait a minute," said Victor. "That phone call at Ernie's that made Ben go crazy—that must have been the Emperor calling." He filled Jaime in.

"I'm sure that was him," she agreed. "And it sounds like he hasn't given up trying to control Ben. We have to make absolutely sure that never happens."

"Don't worry," volunteered Scott. "We turned off the phone."

"That won't be enough," said Jaime. "One of our Custodians has connections. We'll make sure your number can't be traced to your home."

"I never thought of that," said Victor.

"Of course you didn't," said Jaime. "Now we need to go on the attack. It's time to do some investigating at the Right Cycle Company."

"Do you think that's wise?" asked Victor. "We know the Emperor is still trying to control Ben. Maybe one of the other Custodians should go."

"The other Custodians—what's left of them—are guarding their own inventors. I'd go myself, but I have my hands full working for the Underground. But you're right about Dr. Franklin. He should stay far away from that place."

Franklin nodded. "If not me, then who?"

Jaime sighed. "I can't believe I'm saying this, but it has to be these two."

"We could call the police," said Scott. "Or the army."

"We can't trust anyone. As it is, the mayor and several important officials appear to be under the Emperor's control." Jaime glanced at her watch. "I have to go. I've been here too long already."

"How do we report back to you?" asked Victor.

"Take this," said Jaime. She handed Victor a cell phone. "Call the number in the address book, leave a message, then destroy the phone. When the time is right, I'll contact you. Until then, you're on your own." She stood up. "Dr. Franklin, it's been an honor."

"Godspeed, Jaime. Please send my regards to the other Custodians."

Jaime pulled her hood up over her head and slipped out the door.

"She seems nice," said Scott.

"It is good to know the Order survives," agreed Franklin. "Although it sounds like we have much work to do. What is our next move?"

"I hate to say it," said Victor, "but Scott and I need to pay the Wright brothers another visit."

CHAPTER THIRTEEN
The Secret of the Wright Brothers

Victor followed Scott through the window and dropped down onto the warehouse floor. He surveyed the immense room.

"It's all gone!" whispered Scott. Where there had once been mountains of disassembled bicycle parts, only a few scattered piles remained. "Where did it go?"

Victor looked around the room. "That freight elevator—I bet they took everything upstairs."

Scott ran over to the elevator. "Should I push the button?"

"Definitely not," said Victor, examining a pile of reflectors and fenders. "We're here to collect evidence, then get out before we get caught. Just take pictures of everything you see, and I'll make notes. Got it? Scott?"

Victor looked around. Where had Scott gone?

"Up here!" Scott shouted from the top of a metal staircase.

"*Shhh!* Someone will hear you!"

"Come on up! I found a door."

Victor hesitated. Whatever the Wright brothers were up to was probably going on upstairs. Reluctantly, he climbed the staircase.

"It's locked," said Scott, yanking the doorknob.

"Give me a minute." Victor pulled a case from his pocket and knelt by the keyhole. He opened the case and selected two stainless-steel tools: a thin tension wrench and an L-rake lock pick.

Thirty seconds and one soft click later, he turned the knob and eased the door open a crack.

"Nice!" Scott whispered, impressed.

Cautiously, Victor pulled the door open a little more and peeked inside. He could hear two faint voices, masked by a loud hissing noise.

"What do you see?" Scott asked.

"I can sort of hear them, but I can't see a thing," Victor said. "A bunch of crates are in the way."

"If we can't see them, they can't see us, right?" Scott pushed past Victor and skittered up against the stack of crates. He looked back at Victor and waved him in.

Victor took a deep breath and crawled across the rough

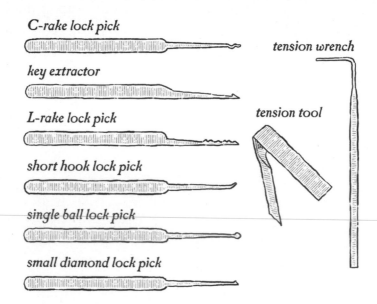

C-rake lock pick

tension wrench

key extractor

L-rake lock pick

tension tool

short hook lock pick

single ball lock pick

small diamond lock pick

wooden floor to where Scott was hiding. The hissing grew louder.

"That was crazy!" Victor said. "If they'd seen you—"

Scott peered over the top of a crate. "I think they're too busy to notice. Look."

Victor peeked between two crates. He and Scott were at the edge of another enormous room, as large as the one downstairs. At the center stood the Wright brothers. Orville hunched over a table staring intently at some large papers—blueprints, Victor guessed. Beside him, Wilbur operated a blowtorch that hissed flames, welding a section of a monstrous metal contraption. Forty feet long and almost as wide, it was constructed of countless bicycle chains, sprockets, and frames welded together into a terrifying skeletal system.

Wilbur twisted a valve on an acetylene tank and shut off the torch. Orville helped his brother stretch a long piece of canvas across the top of the contraption, fastening it to the framework.

"They're making wings," Scott whispered. "It's a giant bat!"

"That's no bat," Victor said. "They're the Wright brothers. It's a giant *bat plane!*"

Orville and Wilbur cocked their heads. Victor clamped his hand over his mouth, and the boys ducked down behind the crate. Two sets of footsteps approached and stopped close by. Victor and Scott held their breaths. After a few tense seconds, the footsteps tip-tapped away and the boys exhaled in relief.

The brothers returned to the plane. Wilbur worked quickly and efficiently, connecting a clear hose to an engine, while Orville opened the valve on a large vat. Glowing blue liquid began flowing through the hose.

Victor recognized it instantly—*harmonic fluid!*

As it surged from the vat to the engine, the brothers gazed at it, as if drawn to the radiant liquid inside.

Scott pointed across the room. "If we can sneak over

there, we can get a better look."

Before Victor could stop him, Scott had slipped farther into the room, ducking behind a new set of crates. Scott snapped a few pictures of the bat plane. Victor silently counted to three and then dashed to Scott's side.

From their new position, they could see two smaller planes. These were completely assembled and painted black. Their wings were curved with a scalloped edge along the back. Each plane looked big enough to carry just one person.

"I get it now," Victor whispered. "When people reported seeing giant bats around the city, they were actually seeing these things."

"So why are they building an even bigger one?"

Victor thought for a moment. "Maybe the small ones are prototypes."

"Proto-whats?" Scott asked.

"Prototypes," Victor explained. "Early models of an invention that can be tested and improved upon. They must have built the smaller ones so they could figure out how to build that giant one. But why?"

Scott pointed past Victor's shoulder. "Oh, man—look at that!"

A semicircle of five people were seated in a corner of the room, their backs against a strange machine. Victor gasped.

"It's okay," Scott said. "I don't think they can see us."

Victor looked closer. The people's eyes were open, but they stared blankly into space, as still as statues. Victor recognized all five of them from the news: Mayor Milstead, Police Chief Hawkins, WURP reporter Katie Kaitlyn, Mr. Girard from the FAA, and Dr. Kane, the zoologist.

Victor and Scott cautiously approached the five people. A relay of clear tubing pumped blue fluid into their necks.

"Yuck!" said Scott.

"More harmonic fluid," said Victor. "Strange."

The machine behind them hummed and pulsated eerily. It looked like a stack of steel and glass inner tubes, and was topped with an antenna that projected up through a hole in the ceiling. Every few seconds, the hum grew louder and the people sat up straight. When the hum softened, they relaxed again.

"Is the machine making them do that?" Scott asked.

"Sure looks like it. Jaime said that the Emperor was controlling the Wright brothers. I'll bet he's using this machine to command these people too."

"How?"

"Those tubes leading to their necks must be injecting them with the harmonic fluid. Maybe the Emperor uses it to hypnotize them or something."

"Creepy," Scott said. "Like a remote control—for humans!"

"Exactly. And that would explain why the mayor and these officials said there weren't any giant bats. They were under the Emperor's power."

"It's like this movie I saw where people were taken over by plants from outer space, and they all became pod people!" Scott said. "So how do we get them out of here?"

Victor considered the question. "We can't. Not yet. We're just here to collect information."

"But won't they—hang on a second . . ."

"What?"

"Dust. I'm gonna sneeze . . ."

"No!" Victor looked around. He snatched up a sheet of paper from the top of the crate and shoved it in front of Scott's face.

"*Aaaaaaa-CHOOO!* Phew! Thanks." Scott wiped his nose with the paper and stuffed it into his pocket.

Victor peered over the crate at the Wright brothers. They hadn't heard.

He rifled through the papers on the crate. "Hey, check out these plans!"

"Uh, Victor?"

"They're blueprints of their giant plane. This could be the key to everything."

"Victor! They're waking up!"

Chief Hawkins was the first to rise, followed by Katie Kaitlyn. One by one, they all stood, tottering from side to side like zombies, their eyes fixated on Victor and Scott. Mayor Milstead raised her arm, pointed at the boys, and shrieked.

A siren blared from above. Lights flashed. Victor looked up and saw a security camera swiveling directly over their heads. Far at the other end of the long room, the Wright brothers turned in alarm.

"Run!" Scott shouted, already halfway to the door.

Victor grabbed an armful of blueprints and dashed for the exit as Scott disappeared through the doorway just ahead.

Fwoooooosh!

Suddenly, Orville Wright stood before him, blocking the door.

"How did you—?" Victor gasped for breath. "You . . . you were way back there!"

Orville grasped a strange device, the size of an electric razor. Two long, sharp needles extended from it. Orville drew closer and aimed it at Victor's throat.

"No!" Victor scrambled back.

Fwoooooosh!

Wilbur stood behind him. Like Orville, he also clutched a double-needle device.

"You should not have come here." Wilbur's voice was low and menacing.

"Prepare to join us," Orville said, pressing a button on the device. The needles began to hum.

"Hey, vampires—say cheese!"

There was a bright flash. Orville and Wilbur dropped their weapons and staggered back, shielding their eyes.

Flash! Flash! Flash!

Scott shot three more pictures. "Come *on,* Victor!"

Victor and Scott sprinted for the door and slammed it shut behind them.

Thunk!

Two sharp needles pierced the wooden door inches from Victor's ear.

Scott shot down the stairs. Victor scrambled behind. Ten steps down, his foot slipped and he tumbled the rest of the way. He landed flat on his back, and the blueprints scattered all over the floor.

Victor groaned and looked up. The brothers were standing at the top of the stairs, brandishing their weapons.

Fighting the pain, Victor clambered out the window. As he hung from the sill, he suddenly remembered the blueprints on the floor. They were too important to leave behind.

Fwoooooooshhhhh!

The Wright brothers stood at the window, inches from Victor's face. He let go of the windowsill and dropped to the pavement below.

THUNK! THUNK!

Above, the needles punctured the windowsill. Blue harmonic fluid splashed into the air.

"Run!" Victor yelled to Scott. "Really, really fast!"

As they tore down the alley, Victor glanced back to see the Wright brothers watching from the window, shielding their eyes from the midday sun.

CHAPTER FOURTEEN
Reading Between the Lines

"*And that machine* you saw," Franklin said, from across the kitchen table. "Why do you suppose it controlled only those people? Why not everyone in the city?"

"I think I know," said Victor. "When I was climbing out the window, one of the brothers came at me with a strange weapon. It had two needles for injecting harmonic fluid. My theory is that's how the Emperor has taken control of them."

"By shooting it into their necks," Scott added. "Vampire style!"

"I'm still not sure I understand," said Franklin. "How exactly does the harmonic fluid give him control?"

"Remember when we tried to use your body as an

antenna for the electrophone?" Victor said. "This is the same idea."

"I see," said Franklin. "When the brothers inject harmonic fluid into people's bodies, that makes them into antennas too."

Victor snapped his fingers. "And I just remembered something else. At the warehouse, the noise that giant machine was making sounded a lot like the noise that came out of my phone."

"But my grandfather's radio didn't make that noise," said Scott.

"No, it didn't. But it did fall into the harmonic fluid. It could be sending a different signal, like static, that drives Ben and the Wright brothers crazy."

"Then the machine at the warehouse—and the cell phone call at Ernie's—were broadcasting something more specific," Franklin said grimly. "Instructions from the Emperor that cannot be disobeyed."

"So if those needles had hit us," Scott asked, "then we would have been under his control too?"

Victor gulped.

"It's brilliant in its own depraved way," Franklin admitted. "First the Emperor took control of the Wright brothers, then used *them* to take over others. One shudders to imagine his next move."

"After we got far enough away from the warehouse," Victor said, "I called the number on Jaime's cell phone and left a message reporting what we'd seen."

"Then I smashed the phone with a brick," Scott said. "It was awesome!"

"That might explain the communication I received," Franklin said. "In all the excitement, it slipped my mind. Just before you arrived, the electrophone began broadcasting again."

Victor sat up straight. "What did it say?"

Franklin looked around the kitchen cautiously.

"No words," Franklin said. "Only letters and numbers. I would estimate the broadcast lasted only ten minutes before ceasing entirely. I was fortunate to be in the lab at the time."

He reached into a pocket and pulled out a folded piece of paper. "I'm no stranger to puzzles, but I've gone over this a dozen times and admit that I am baffled."

He handed the slip of paper to Victor, who unfolded it and read,

"$C_6H_8O_7$."

"Maybe it's another code," Scott suggested.

"This is no code, it's a chemical formula," Victor said. He switched on his phone and connected to the Internet. "Yup, citric acid. The stuff in oranges. Why would Jaime send this?"

The front door opened. "Hi, boys," Mrs. Godwin said. She dropped her gardening trowel into the sink and reached into her back pocket. "Victor, a girl handed me this flyer a few minutes ago. She told me you'd asked for information about summer volunteer work. Good for you."

"Really?" Victor said. He glanced at the paper. The heading read "Maintain Our Parks."

"Mr. Benjamin, I need to run down to the store for some of those new lightbulbs. Do you mind keeping an eye on the boys?"

"Not at all," Franklin replied.

After she left, Victor put the flyer on the table for the others to see. "Here's another piece of our puzzle."

"What do you mean?" Scott asked.

"Don't you see?" Victor said. "Maintain Our Parks—M-O-P. This must be a message from the Order. And that girl must have been Jaime."

Victor read it aloud.

"Moms, dads, brothers and sisters!

"Please help us with our plan to control litter in Fairmount Park! Everyone in Philadelphia is invited to help us clean it up this Wednesday, from morning until night, using whatever tools you have at hand. Rain clouds or sunny skies, we'll be there.

"Be sure to stop by the registration tent at Lemon Hill Mansion to sign in. And don't forget your glove and bat. Afterward, we'll celebrate with a softball game and a recycled paper airplane contest.

"Thanks for your help. Philadelphia needs you!

"What a strange message," Victor said. "Why did she hand-deliver it?"

"Yeah, she could have just called," Scott said. "You know, on the electrophone."

"She did call on the electrophone," Franklin reminded him. "The question is, how are the two messages related?"

Victor placed the chemical formula on the table next to the flyer. "Now, that's interesting."

"What do you see, my boy?" Franklin asked.

"The letter mentions the mansion at Fairmount Park—Lemon Hill. Oranges aren't the only fruits that contain citric acid. Lemons do too. I think that's a hint. Come here!"

Franklin and Scott followed Victor to a lamp. Victor removed the lamp shade and flicked the switch. He held the letter over the hot lightbulb.

"If you dip a toothpick in lemon juice and write on paper," Victor explained, "it dries clear. But the citric acid in the juice weakens the paper slightly. Then, when it's held over heat, the invisible writing turns brown."

"Invisible ink," Franklin said. "Of course!"

They stared at the paper as dark lines began to appear beneath certain words.

TOOTHPICK

✪ ✪ ✪

MOMS, DADS, BROTHERS AND SISTERS!

Please help us with our plan to control litter in Fairmount Park! Everyone in Philadelphia is invited to help us clean it up this Wednesday, from morning until night, using whatever tools you have at hand. Rain clouds or sunny skies, we'll be there.

Be sure to stop by the registration tent at Lemon Hill Mansion to sign in. And don't forget your glove and bat. Afterward, we'll celebrate with a softball game and a recycled paper airplane contest.

✪ ✪ ✪

Thanks for your help.
Philadelphia needs you!

Victor removed the letter from the hot bulb and handed it to Franklin.

"This is terrible," Franklin said, frowning. He read the secret message aloud.

"Brothers plan to control everyone in Philadelphia this Wednesday night, using rain clouds. Stop the bat airplane. Philadelphia needs you!"

INVISIBLE INK INSTRUCTIONS

Materials needed: lemon juice, a toothpick or thin paintbrush, some paper, and a lamp with a lightbulb.

1. Squeeze some lemon juice into a cup.

2. Dip the tip of your toothpick or paintbrush into the juice.

3. Write your secret message on the paper.

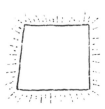

4. Let the juice dry. It will become invisible!

5: To reveal the hidden message, hold the paper over a (warm) lightbulb.

TIPS:

Other liquids will also work as invisible ink, including apple juice and vinegar.

For greater secrecy, first compose your message using a code or cipher before writing it on the paper with invisible ink.

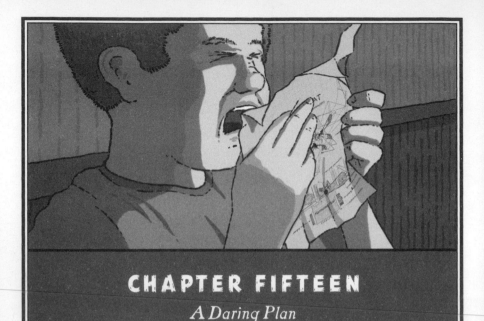

CHAPTER FIFTEEN
A Daring Plan

"Rain clouds?" Scott said. "How are they going to use rain clouds to control everyone?"

"How indeed?" Franklin mused. "The brothers have already demonstrated that they can control people, but only on an individual basis. This must be the next step in their plan."

"We need to know more about that bat airplane," Victor said. "If we can find its weakness, we might be able to—"

"Aaaa-choo!" Scott sneezed into the crook of his arm. "Excuse me." He sniffled. "Dust."

"One of these days, I shall have to give this laboratory a thorough cleaning." Franklin searched his jacket. "I'm afraid I haven't a handkerchief for you."

"That's okay," Scott said. He reached into his pocket, found a piece of paper, and brought it up to his nose.

"Hold it!" Victor shouted. "That piece of paper—"

"It's okay," Scott said. "I only used it once. The other side's clean."

"No, that's not it. Please, just lay it out on the table."

Scott sniffled and unfolded the paper. The page was covered in words, numbers, and diagrams.

"Blueprints from the warehouse!" Victor said.

"Sure. You gave it to me when I had to sneeze. Hey, it's a drawing of that bat airplane thing."

"A stroke of luck," Franklin said, adjusting his bifocals.

A diagram of the large bat airplane filled most of the page. Written above it was the word *Megabat*. At the bottom, the diagram depicted a large tank suspended beneath the Megabat with a dozen spray nozzles sticking out of it. The words *Harmonic Fluid* were written to the side of the tank.

"Jaime said that the Wright brothers would use clouds to control everyone," Franklin said. "They must mean to use harmonic fluid to poison the rain! It pains me to think that Promethean inventors could be capable of such evil."

"But remember, the Wright brothers aren't really responsible," Victor said. "It's the Emperor. They're just under his control."

"Who *is* this Emperor anyway?" Scott asked.

"We don't know," Franklin said. "But now that he knows

MEGABAT

Harmonic Distribution System (HDS)

hydraulic derailleur •

• release lever

• main pump gear assembly

charging vents •

Harmonic Fluid

• pressurizing wheel

• ionizing intake assembly

• distribution nozzles

who *we* are, that makes him even more dangerous."

"So how do we stop him?" Victor said. "The Wright brothers are going to strike in just a few days. It's too risky to return to the bicycle factory."

"It is risky to go most anywhere," Franklin said. "The Emperor is sure to be watching. We must plan our next steps carefully."

He stood and paced the laboratory floor.

"If we can't reach the airplane while it's inside the warehouse," reasoned Franklin, "then we will have to wait until it is out in the open, on the evening of their plan."

"Won't that be cutting it kind of close?" Scott asked.

"I think Ben's right," said Victor. "It's our only option. But even once it's out in the open, how will we stop it?"

"We could use a net," Scott suggested. "That's how my dad catches bats in our attic. If we had a giant butterfly net, we could grab them when they fly by."

"Scott, *please*," said Victor. "We're trying to think."

"Now, now, Victor. Scott might be on to something." Franklin leaned in. "What if we *could* build a net? Could we make it strong enough to bring down the Megabat?"

"It's ridiculous," said Victor. "We can't make a net that big. And even if we could, there's no way we could make it strong enough. The Megabat would fly right through it."

"But you're forgetting," Franklin said, "their airplane will be carrying a massive tank of harmonic fluid. That means it may be susceptible to an overdose of electricity, just like me. What if we were to invent an *electric* net?"

"Yeah, that's what I meant!" Scott said. "An electric net!"

Victor shook his head. "For one thing, to bring down the Megabat we'd need a phenomenal amount of electricity. Where would that come from? And besides, how would we get the net in the air? It's crazy."

"If I didn't know better," said Franklin, with a wink, "I'd say you were telling us to go fly a kite."

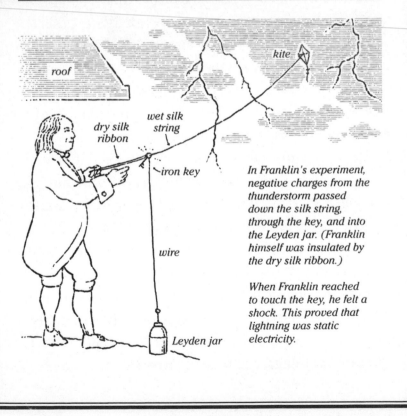

BENJAMIN FRANKLIN'S KITE EXPERIMENT

kite

roof

dry silk ribbon

wet silk string

iron key

wire

Leyden jar

In Franklin's experiment, negative charges from the thunderstorm passed down the silk string, through the key, and into the Leyden jar. (Franklin himself was insulated by the dry silk ribbon.)

When Franklin reached to touch the key, he felt a shock. This proved that lightning was static electricity.

CHAPTER SIXTEEN
The Man in the Silver Suit

An hour later, Ben, Victor, and Scott were studying a crude diagram on the chalkboard. It was a combination of Franklin's inventiveness and Victor's knowledge of modern-day technology. For his part, Scott had contributed several cartoon drawings of vampire bats floating in the sky above.

"Okay," said Victor, "suppose we do manage to build this electrified net of kites. The weather forecast calls for rain showers but not thunderstorms. Without lightning, we can't electrify the net."

"Then we shall have to create it ourselves," Franklin said.

"Create lightning?" Victor said. "How?"

"My dad is a meteorologist," said Scott. "He knows tons about lightning."

Victor sighed. "Don't take this the wrong way, Scott, but this is a little out of his league. We'd need a real meteorologist."

"My dad *is* a meteorologist."

"Scott—"

"You don't know him, Victor. He's the best there is. He just does that funny stuff to make the weather more fun to watch."

Franklin chuckled in agreement. "Your father certainly is fun to watch."

"This isn't about having fun," said Victor. He turned back to the diagram on the board. "Now, do you think your father could put us in touch with the guy who does the morning forecast? What's his name . . . Jason something?"

"Look, Victor." Scott stood up, his face reddening. "I always do what you say. You're the smart one. But this time you're wrong. Just because my dad puts on a show doesn't make him a bad weatherman."

"He mispronounced *Arkansas* in his forecast last week."

"Everybody makes mistakes," said Scott. "Even you. Remember your volcano?"

Victor winced at the memory of his science project run amok. "This is hardly the same thing. We can't trust this operation to a man who dresses like a giant bicycle seat."

"You think he likes doing that?" Scott shot back. "If the

stupid station wasn't making him pay for the camera—"

"That *he* broke, riding that scooter instead of delivering the forecast like a normal weatherman—"

"Gentlemen, please!" Franklin stepped between the two boys. "I think it best we pause for a moment and collect ourselves. This is no time for arguments."

"You take it back, Victor. Say my dad's an awesome weatherman, or I'm leaving."

Victor turned to Franklin. "Ben, you see what I'm getting at, don't you?"

"No, Victor," Franklin said sternly. "I do not."

"You can't be serious!"

"I am perfectly serious. While I understand your concerns about the technical side of our plan, you have forgotten something even more important. We need someone we can trust. If Mr. Weaver's character is anything like that of his son, he is exactly the person we need."

"But—"

"Scott, we will need to speak to your father right away. Is he home?"

"He's working right now," said Scott. "But I know where to find him."

Halfway across the Buy-and-Buy parking lot, Victor began to get a bad feeling. He could see the crowd gathered at the entrance, hooting and cheering. What kind of spectacle was Skip Weaver making of himself this time?

It was even worse than he had imagined. There was Skip, dressed in a skintight silvery spandex suit. He was more than just a little overweight, and the suit highlighted every fold and wrinkle of his doughy frame.

Skip's belly, thighs, and arms were tethered with cloth belts to a large, motorized wheel mounted on a tripod. When Skip pressed a button, the wheel spun violently back and forth, shaking his entire body as if he were being electrocuted.

"Step right up, folks! Nothing to be afraid of," called Skip, his voice vibrating with the machine. "We call this beauty the Slimshaker Five Thousand. Take it from me, your weatherman, Skip Weaver: with this machine, the forecast calls for sunny skies and a slimmer you."

"Ingenious!" said Franklin.

"Anyone here struggle with thunder thighs?" continued Skip. "This machine cures 'em as fast as lightning!"

"Do you think it hurts?" asked Scott.

"I'm sure it does," said Victor. "And it probably doesn't even work."

Skip patted his belly. "If you folks are like me, you may have noticed a large front moving in." The crowd laughed in agreement. "My professional advice? Stay off the roads—and fix that spare tire with the Slimshaker Five Triple Zero!"

Victor groaned. "That doesn't even make sense."

"Shall we purchase one?" asked Franklin, patting his own belly.

Fifteen minutes later, the four of them had gathered around coffee and doughnuts inside the Buy-and-Buy.

"So you see, Mr. Weaver," explained Victor, "it's a very delicate experiment Mr. Benjamin is attempting here. Due to, er . . . patent issues, it's critical that we keep the whole thing secret."

"Got It," said Skip with a wink. He turned to Franklin. "And what do you need me for?"

"It is quite simple, really," said Franklin. "We need to create lightning from scratch—just a single strike, you understand—and we are not sure how to do it. We were hoping you could help."

"Is that all?" Skip laughed. "Create lightning? You're out of your mind. Seriously, what's this all about?"

"I assure you, we are perfectly serious," said Franklin.

Skip Weaver stood up and dusted the doughnut crumbs off his silvery suit. "Look, fellows, this has been fun, but I've got to get back to work. What you're asking for is impossible. Sorry I couldn't be more help."

"I knew we should have called a real meteorologist," muttered Victor.

warm air

positive charge

negative charge

Lightning gets its start when warm air rises.

As the air goes higher into the sky, it cools. The cooling causes the invisible water vapor inside to condense into little drops.

This forms a cloud.

As the drops of water get colder, some of them freeze.

All the while, they move around and bump into each other. This creates a charge in the cloud.

The top of the cloud has a positive charge. The bottom has a negative charge.

The ground below the cloud has a positive charge.

When the ground's positive charge and the cloud's negative charge get strong enough, they pull toward each other.

Lightning is born!

Skip spun around. "Excuse me? I *am* a real meteorologist," he said, pulling up his hood, "and I'm telling you it can't be done, no way, no how."

"Mr. Weaver," pleaded Franklin, "I know our request must sound absurd, but I beg of you to give us one moment more. Theoretically, if resources were no object, what might it take to induce lightning? In your professional opinion as a premier scientist, of course."

Skip paused, considering Franklin's words. Then he sat back down. "Okay, you want to create lightning from scratch? First you'll need to create a lot, and I mean *a lot,* of really warm air. How do you do that? I have no idea. Then you'll have to get this warm air up to about thirty thousand feet, really fast. And then, if you want to draw the lightning to the ground, you'll need something really high to attract the strike."

"Like a kite?" offered Franklin.

"Sure, a kite," said Skip quizzically. "Who do you think you are, Ben Franklin?"

"You flatter me," said Franklin. "Now, there's much more we need to discuss. I cannot go into specifics, except to say that your ideas may be more feasible than you realize. Might we continue our conversation this evening?"

"Mr. Benjamin," whispered Victor, "are you sure you want to do this?"

"Positive, my boy. Mr. Weaver, shall we say eight o'clock at my lodgings? I promise it will be worth your while."

"Please, Dad?" said Scott. "We need you."

"Very well," said Skip, "but I still don't see what good it will do."

"Excellent," Franklin said. He swallowed the last of his doughnut. "On a separate topic, this Slimshaker of yours— may I give it a try?"

CHAPTER SEVENTEEN
The Lightning Engine

"Mr. Weaver," said Franklin, inviting Skip into his apartment, "I am sorry to take up your time this late at night, but I assure you, it is most important."

Skip stepped inside. "Nice place. Lived here long?"

"You could say that," said Franklin with a chuckle. "The boys are waiting for us downstairs."

Franklin led his guest to the bookcase. He gave it a tug, and it swung open. "After you," he offered.

Skip paused, a doubtful expression on his face.

"It's okay, Dad," shouted Scott from below. "Come on down."

Gingerly, Skip stepped onto the ladder and lowered himself into the shaft. A moment later, he found himself standing in the middle of an enormous laboratory filled with antique and modern equipment, all humming and pulsing with a faint blue glow.

"I apologize for the mess," said Franklin. "We've been busy working and haven't had a chance to tidy up."

Skip's expression transformed into one of utter confusion. "How . . . I mean where . . . What is this place?"

"This is my, or rather, *our* laboratory," said Franklin, gesturing to Victor and Scott. "If you'd like to have a seat, I think I can explain everything."

Franklin led Skip to a stool and sat him down. "I know from your son that you are a man of good character. I feel we can trust you with our secret."

"Secret?" said Skip. "What's this all about, Mr. Benjamin?"

Franklin sat down on a stool and pulled it close. "Perhaps that is a good place to start. You see, my name is not Mr. Benjamin. Rather, it is Mr. *Franklin . . .*"

With Victor and Scott's help, Franklin brought Skip Weaver up to speed on the Modern Order of Prometheus, the Great Emergency, the Wright brothers, and the lightning net.

"You guys have to understand," Skip said apologetically, "this is a lot to take in. Why exactly am I here again?"

"You're here, Dad," said Scott, "because we need to make lightning, and only you know how to do it."

Skip shook his head. "I told you, buddy—it can't be done."

"Not exactly," said Franklin. "You told us it *could* be done, but you didn't know how. We're hoping that maybe, with all of us working together, we can solve that second part."

"The big problem is the heat," said Skip. "You'd need a tremendous amount of power to generate it."

Franklin gestured to several large machines behind him. "As it happens, generating power is something we know how to do. And as for heat, perhaps you've heard of the Franklin stove?"

"Sure, but what does that have to do with—" He suddenly remembered who he was talking to. "Oh, right. But even if you could generate the heat, you'd need to aim it upward, almost like a cannon."

THE FRANKLIN STOVE

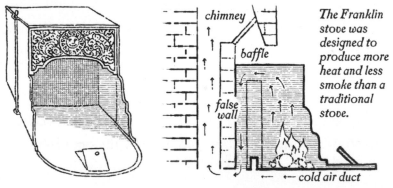

chimney

baffle

false wall

cold air duct

The Franklin stove was designed to produce more heat and less smoke than a traditional stove.

"You're talking about focused heat projection," said Victor. "Ben, isn't that how the Hyperion coiling system works?" He pointed to a large spring leading into the ground at the rear of the laboratory.

"It is," said Franklin. "When lightning strikes the antenna on the roof, excess heat is dissipated down into the earth through those coils."

"Like a radiator," said Scott.

"Exactly," said Victor. "Now, what if we could redirect that coil upward? If we had a big enough charge, it would generate an enormous amount of heat. I've been down here during a thunderstorm, and the temperature in the room rises a good twenty degrees every time the Hyperion coil kicks in."

"Okay," said Skip, "but don't you have this backward? Your coil there generates heat when lightning strikes. But you guys want to *make* lightning with the coil. How are you going to heat it up in the first place?"

"We could plug it in," offered Scott. "Or use lots and lots of batteries."

"Or," said Franklin, pointing to the large metal orb hanging from the ceiling, "we could use just one big battery."

Hours later, the plan was finally starting to take shape. Skip stood at the chalkboard, going over the details.

"The timing on this whole thing is going to be critical," he said. "As soon as the Wright brothers are in view, we'll need to fire the Hyperion coil. That should heat the air directly above us. When the air rises high enough, it will cool and form ice crystals in the cloud tops, generating electricity. We'll have to ionize the kite net right away in order to draw the lightning down."

"What if there isn't any wind?" Scott asked. "How will we get the net in the air?"

"Shouldn't be a problem," Skip explained. "All that heat should create a massive, localized front. We'll be generating our own wind."

Victor couldn't believe it. He was actually *impressed* with Skip Weaver.

"A million things could go wrong, and it will be enormously dangerous. But from what you've told me about this Megabat, we have no other choice."

"Are you are certain you can secure a WURP news van?" Franklin asked.

"Leave it to me," Skip said. "There's an old one out back that they never use anymore."

"Excellent. In the meantime, we shall disassemble the necessary equipment and prepare it for our mission."

"Scott and I will run to Ernie's to get the stuff for the electric kite net," Victor added.

"Good thinking, Victor," Franklin said. "We haven't a moment to spare. Let's get to work."

CHAPTER EIGHTEEN
Baiting the Hook

Victor and Scott hunkered down behind a Dumpster, a block from the Wright brothers' warehouse. Nothing had happened in the hour they had been waiting. A light drizzle began to fall.

Scott's mountain bike leaned against a wall. Victor's own bike was still at the Right Cycle Company, surely by now a piece of the Megabat. He'd had to make do with his mom's old bike—a ladies' pink three-speed that had only one working gear.

"You've triple-checked the radio, right?" Victor said. "If it doesn't work, the whole plan falls apart."

Scott patted his grandfather's old radio, which he had crudely duct-taped to his bike's handlebars. "I checked it this morning. Then I dunked it in the harmonic fluid again. You know—for extra harmonica. See anything yet?"

"Not yet."

BRMBRMBRMBRMBRMBRMBRMBRM . . .

"What's that noise?" Victor asked.

"Look!"

Atop the warehouse, two giant hatch doors split open like a drawbridge and clattered flat onto the roof. Slowly, a massive shadowy form rose from within.

Victor peered through the bioptiscope. "The Megabat!"

Despite its evil purpose, it was a stunning achievement. Perhaps forty feet long, the Megabat was black, sleek, and frightening, but in a strange way, Victor found it beautiful. Wilbur Wright turned a large crank, and its four wings, which had been pressed vertically against the fuselage, slowly opened and leveled off.

"Let me see," Scott said. Victor handed him the bioptiscope. "Holy cow! That is *so cool*."

Wilbur turned another crank.

TICKA-TICKA-TICKA-TICKA-TICKA . . .

The platform beneath the Megabat tilted up at a forty-five-degree angle, pointing the plane's nose into the night sky. Now Victor could see the tank of harmonic fluid suspended beneath. He shivered at the thought of the mayhem it would cause should the Emperor's terrible plan succeed.

Orville and Wilbur slowly walked around the plane, inspecting it. Dressed in black, their bodies blended into

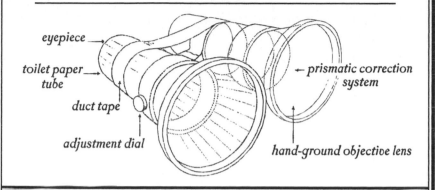

eyepiece

toilet paper tube

duct tape

adjustment dial

← prismatic correction system

hand-ground objective lens

the night. Victor turned a dial on the bioptiscope and zoomed in on the brothers' heads. Their ashen faces stood out boldly against the darkness around them.

Victor gulped. They *did* look like vampires.

The brothers climbed onto the lower wing and lay down beside each other on their stomachs.

"It's almost time," Victor said. "Get ready."

The Megabat began to rumble, its propellers spinning wildly. The boys hopped onto their bikes.

"Switch it on," Victor directed.

Scott hit the switch on his grandfather's radio. Nothing happened.

"Turn it on, Scott!"

"I'm trying," Scott said. "It's not doing anything."

"Well, try again! They're about to take off."

The propellers whirred louder. There was a clang, and the Megabat launched into the air and began to soar away.

Within seconds, it would surely be out of range. Victor tried to keep himself from panicking. "Scott!"

"I just thought of something," Scott said. "See if this helps."

He turned the volume knob all the way up. A horrible static blared from the radio.

"Fixed it!"

But were they in time?

Victor and Scott scanned the skies. The Megabat was already gone.

"We're too late." Victor sighed. "We missed our chance."

Then came the buzz. First soft, then steadily louder.

"There it is!" Scott yelled.

A giant bat-shaped silhouette swooped low. For one horrible second, it seemed to fill the sky. Then, with an acrobatic roll, it vanished from sight.

"Let's move!" commanded Victor. The boys tore down the street.

Suddenly, the Wright brothers reappeared, circling high above in their terrifying machine, banking and swirling.

"It's working!" Scott screamed, pouring on more speed. "They're coming at us!"

The Megabat plunged into a steep dive. A bone-chilling scream pierced the air.

As he struggled to keep pace with Scott, Victor huffed into his cell phone headset. "Ben . . . Mr. Weaver . . . they've taken the bait. Fire up the Hyperion coil!"

CHAPTER NINETEEN
Sky Chase

"Faster!" Victor hollered. They sped down alleys and side streets too narrow for the Wright brothers to fly through. The boys had planned their route carefully. As long as they stayed away from major roads, they would be safe.

High above, the Megabat zigged and zagged like a monstrous mosquito.

Skip Weaver's voice crackled in Victor's headset. *"The coil's at optimum temperature . . . Raise the kite, Dr. Franklin!"*

Victor and Scott paused at the end of an alley to catch their breaths.

"We'll have to cross this street fast," Victor said. "As soon as we're out in the open, we'll be exposed."

The streetlight turned green. They each took a deep breath and kicked off, speeding across the intersection. Victor looked up to find the Megabat close behind, flying so low that he could see the confused madness on the brothers' faces.

Static hissed in Victor's earphone: *". . . wires are snapping . . . going back . . ."*

Going back? What was Ben talking about?

Victor heard Skip's voice shout back. *"No! . . . too dangerous . . . be killed!"*

The boys steered their bikes into the next alley. "Mr. Weaver! . . . Ben! . . . We're almost there! Is everything all right?"

"No!" Skip shouted. *"There's a problem! The kite net—"*

"There is no problem!" Franklin insisted. *"Proceed as planned!"*

Victor felt the air temperature rising and the wind picking up. The Hyperion coil was evidently up and running.

The boys careened into the next alley. Victor spotted the chain-link fence at the edge of the Arthur Parker Art Park. The park had been the perfect place to set their trap: full of wide-open spaces, secluded, and devoid of people. They skidded their bikes to a stop and dragged them under the fence.

"This way," Scott shouted. "Past the giant nose!"

They hopped back on their bikes and took off across the park, swerving between the enormous sculptures on

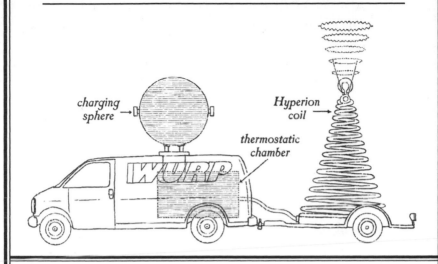

their way to the trap. The Megabat's propellers buzzed close behind.

At the crest of the next hill, Victor breathed a quick sigh of relief. The old WURP news van was parked in position. Next to it, the Hyperion coil fired ripples of heat into the sky, where dark clouds were forming. Dozens of box kites lurched violently in the wind, tethered by a nearly invisible web of wire to—

Victor's stomach tensed as they pedaled closer. There *was* a problem.

Franklin teetered atop the news van, his foot hooked beneath the giant orb. He clutched the frayed ends of the kite net with both hands as it thrashed and snapped in the wind.

"*Dr. Franklin,*" Skip called, "*I can't throw the switch until you're clear of the net. You'll be electrocuted!*"

Victor screamed into his headset. "He's right! It's too dangerous!"

"*If I let go of the net, it will blow away,*" Franklin insisted. "*Victor! Scott! Lure them this way!*"

They had no choice. The Megabat was gaining on them. Thirty feet from the van, Victor veered left as Scott veered right. They converged on the other side and pedaled on. Victor turned to see the Megabat swoop down at them. It was working. The brothers hadn't seen the net!

"*Now!*" Franklin shouted.

"*But you'll—*"

"*NOW!*" Franklin commanded. "*NOW!*"

Skip threw the switch. Lightning cracked in the sky, struck the kite net, and raced down the wire through the Megabat, through Franklin, and into the orb.

"*Rrrarrrrrrrrrrrrggghhhhhh!*" Franklin howled.

The Megabat thrashed in the net like a fish on a line. Flames rose from its wings, and Franklin was yanked into the air. The plane tumbled across the sky, towing him behind.

Victor gazed on in shock as the Megabat, the Wright brothers, and Franklin crashed over a distant hill.

He felt a strong hand on his shoulder. "Get in the van," Skip Weaver commanded. "Dr. Franklin needs our help."

CHAPTER TWENTY
Battle Royale

Weighted down with the extra equipment, the old van groaned as it climbed the hill. Mr. Weaver coaxed it along, shifting into a lower gear and pumping the gas pedal.

Clanging and crushing noises echoed from over the crest.

"What's that sound?" Scott asked.

"Rrrrrrraaaaaarrrrrrrrrrrrggggghhh!"

"It's Ben!" Victor said. "He's still alive!"

The van stalled out at the top of the hill. Below them a furious battle was raging.

Franklin and the Wright brothers clashed atop a flaming mountain of glowing, twisted metal that had once been the Megabat. The tank of harmonic fluid had ruptured, and blue liquid flooded the lawn. Orville ripped a chunk of steel from the mangled mess beneath him and flung it at Franklin. With the back of his hand, Franklin swatted it from the air and sent it hurtling upward. Fifty feet away, it struck an enormous steel sculpture of a toothbrush and crashed to the ground.

Victor started to jump out of the van and run to Franklin's aid, but Mr. Weaver held him back. "It's too dangerous."

He knew Mr. Weaver was right. Franklin, the Wright brothers, and the entire wreckage of the Megabat glowed with raw harmonic energy. Franklin was in a supercharged state, and judging by their strength, the brothers were too.

Wilbur tore a bicycle frame from the flaming mountain and swung it. Franklin ducked and stormed at Orville, lifting him into the air. With a roar, he hurled Orville at Wilbur, knocking both brothers onto their backs.

"We have to do something," Victor said. "They'll destroy each other."

"It's too bad we can't just pull out their batteries," Scott said.

Batteries?

"The orb!" Victor exclaimed.

"Of course," Skip said, eyeing the charging sphere on top of the van. "That thing sucks up energy, right?"

"It's like an electric sponge," Victor said. "If we can get them to touch it, it might absorb their power."

Atop the mountain of wreckage, the Wright brothers double-teamed Franklin. One held his neck while the other rammed his stomach with a chunk of the Megabat's engine. Franklin howled and fell to the ground.

"Stand back, boys," Skip directed. He hopped into the van and turned the key. The engine spat and sputtered, then rumbled to life.

Skip turned the wheel toward the glowing wreckage and stepped on the accelerator. The van lurched down the hill and began to pick up speed. He threw open the door and jumped free, tumbling across the grass.

The van hurtled across the lawn and smashed into the wreckage of the Megabat. The impact snapped the orb free from the roof and it rolled onto the towering pile. A trail of sparks shot up the mountain of glowing metal and through the bodies of the men struggling on top. The orb surged, and the harmonic energy began to flow into it like a fountain in reverse.

"It's working!" said Scott.

There was a blinding flash and an earsplitting crack. Victor felt a rippling stream of energy course through his entire body, then everything went dark and silent. Everything except for the orb's pulsating glow.

Once his vision returned, Victor scrambled down the hill, scanning the the pile for any sign of Franklin and the Wright brothers. Franklin's body lay on the far side. The batteries on his belt looked like charcoal briquettes.

"Ben?"

Skip and Scott clambered up behind Victor.

"How is he?" Skip asked.

Victor reached down to check for a pulse but pulled his hand back. "I can't tell. He's too hot to touch."

"His chest isn't moving," Scott said. "He isn't . . . dead, is he?"

A dry wheeze croaked from Franklin's throat. "Reports of my . . . death are . . . greatly exaggerated. Victor, has anyone said that before me? If not, I should like to claim it as my own."

Victor beamed. "Ben, you're alive!"

"Just barely," Franklin said, struggling to sit up. He shook his head. "How did you return me to normal?"

"The orb."

Franklin peered down at the pulsing metal sphere that lay below. "Brilliant work, my boy."

"It was a team effort," said Victor. He turned to Skip. "And Mr. Weaver was awesome."

"Standard celebrity stuff," said Skip.

Franklin chuckled and winced. "Ah, it hurts to laugh. I feel my power is nearly drained. Help me down to the orb, will you? I can use it to restore my energy before we discharge the rest into the sky."

Skip, Scott, and Victor lifted the old man to his feet.

"And the brothers?" Ben asked. "Are they all right?"

"All right?" Skip asked. "They tried to kill you."

"They were not acting of their own accord, Mr. Weaver. They are puppets of the Emperor. If we can help them, we must."

From the other side of the pile came sounds of shifting metal. A silhouette emerged.

"Where . . . am I?"

A second shadowy form followed. "Wilbur?"

"Orville! *Brother!*"

The two men embraced as if they hadn't seen each other in a lifetime.

WRIGHT BROTHERS NATIONAL MEMORIAL, NORTH CAROLINA

CHAPTER TWENTY-ONE
A Second Chance at Life

A week later at the Right Cycle Company, Victor, Scott, and Franklin watched as Orville and Wilbur Wright systematically dismantled the strange doughnut-shaped machine. The last time Victor and Scott had seen it, it had been pumping harmonic fluid into the necks of five of Philadelphia's most influential citizens. According to the brothers, it was called a harmonic transmitter.

Jaime was there, too, taking photographs and making notes. She was still all business, but Victor thought she seemed more relaxed than she had at the diner. At one point, he even caught a glimpse of a smile.

"So what exactly are you going to do with this thing?" asked Victor.

"Step one is to figure out how the transmitter works," said Jaime. "We're hoping some of the Custodians in the Promethean Underground will be able to reverse-engineer it. They're experts in harmonic technology."

"We ourselves only have vague memories of constructing it," Wilbur explained.

"That accursed Emperor's voice!" Orville said. "We just couldn't get it out of our heads. It was maddening."

Victor and Scott helped the brothers pack the dismantled transmitter into several large wooden crates. Jaime carefully recorded each part in her notebook.

"What's going to happen to the other people who were hypnotized?" Scott asked. "Mayor Milstead and the rest. Will they be okay?"

"Powerful though it may be," Franklin said, "harmonic fluid is harmless to the average human body. It will pass through their systems in a day or two."

"That's why the Emperor had to keep them hooked up to that machine," Victor said. "To recharge their harmonic fluid."

"Like at the gas station," Scott said.

"Precisely," Franklin said. "And I speak from experience when I say that once it wears off, they will likely remember nothing."

"Thank goodness," said Jaime. "But what about the wreckage of the Megabat? It's still sitting there in the middle of that art park. Erased memories or not, someone's going to notice."

"We've taken care of it," Victor explained. "Yesterday morning we snuck back and put a plaque in front of it. Ben named it *The Emperor's Spaghetti.*"

Jaime smiled. "I have to hand it to you guys, you really came through. The other members of the Underground can't wait to meet you."

"The feeling is mutual," Franklin said.

"For the first time in quite a while, we feel energized. We may not have won the war, but we've won an important battle."

"True," Franklin said. "But there's no telling whom the Emperor will awaken next. We must remain on our guard."

"Scott," Jaime said, "I wish your dad was here so I could thank him too. I'm glad he's on our side."

"Me too," said Victor. "We couldn't have done it without him. He's a real pro."

"I know!" Scott said. "And wait until you see what he has planned for tomorrow's broadcast. It's going to be windy, so he rented all these fans and he's going to blow everything off the set—even his clothes!"

Victor sighed.

"Delightful!" Franklin said. His face grew serious. "Speaking of parents, Jaime, has there been any news of your own mother and father?"

"Not yet, but there's hope. The Underground believes the Emperor has been abducting Custodians to turn them to his side. With my parents' knowledge of the Order,

THOUGHTFUL PAJAMAS
GEORGE WASHINGTON WITH PORCUPINE
NORMAN ROCKWELL'S LAST POTLUCK SUPPER
FOOD DESCENDING A STAIRCASE
SIR BISCUIT WHISKERS SIPS SOUP
JIGGLING DONKEY

they're more valuable to him alive than dead."

"We'll help you find them," Scott said. "Right, guys?"

"You know it," Victor said.

"It will be my honor," said Franklin. "The Great Emergency is the very reason I am here."

"As are we," added Wilbur. "Although my brother and I will be quite busy over the next few months. It seems we need to reconstruct several hundred bicycles or face some very angry customers."

"In any case, you can count on us," Orville said. "We owe you all a debt of gratitude."

"Agreed," said Wilbur. "The Emperor's voice has been banished from our thoughts. May it never return!"

"The Emperor's voice!" Orville exclaimed. "I suddenly realize where I've heard it before." He staggered to a chair and sat down. "Wilbur, the man who is destroying the Order today is the same man who gave us a second chance at life, so long ago!"

EPILOGUE

"Custodian!" the man screamed. "Come here at once!"

"Yes, Monsier Enbée?" The Custodian raced to the man resting in the large glass and metal casket.

"Why have I lost all contact with the Wright brothers?"

The Custodian trembled. "It appears, sir, that a small network of Custodians—somehow not yet under your control—sabotaged your efforts. We believe that the Modern Order of Prometheus is trying to—"

"I AM THE MODERN ORDER OF PROMETHEUS!" He pounded the top of his Leyden casket. "Curse this box! Once it gave me immortality. Now it confines me like a prison cell."

The Custodian recoiled. Although the little man had

been confined to his Leyden casket for decades, he could still command fear in the bravest of souls. His power seemed boundless.

"Perhaps, sir, we could send a spy to learn what happened to the brothers?"

"It no longer matters," Monsieur Enbée said. "They are lost to me. But thanks to Franklin's inventions, there are other scientists I have already resurrected for my purposes." He picked up a lightbulb from a nearby shelf and idly rolled it between his fingers. "Although I still cannot fathom how Franklin himself escaped my grasp. It had to be the boy."

"They must be stopped, Monsieur Enbée."

"Do not concern yourself with them. I have another plan in the works." He gazed into the lightbulb. "A greater plan."

"Your genius is infinite, Monsieur Enbée!"

"Enough!" the little man shouted from his casket. "I am through hiding behind that false name. From now on, you shall refer to me by my proper title—Napoléon Bonaparte, Emperor of the World!"

CUSTODIANS NEEDED!

Have you ever wondered, "Gee, do I have what it takes to be a Custodian in the Modern Order of Prometheus?" The Order is always on the lookout for promising new recruits. Answer these five simple questions and find out if this job is for you!

1. One of Benjamin Franklin's biggest problems is that when he is overcharged, he becomes a raging monster bent on total destruction. With this in mind, if you were a raging monster bent on total destruction, what would you destroy first?

2.   In the eighteenth century, Benjamin Franklin flew a kite in a thunderstorm as an experiment to determine whether lightning was actually electricity. How nuts was that? Discuss.

3.   Benjamin Franklin created the Modern Order of Prometheus in order to preserve the world's greatest inventors, with the idea of reawakening them one day to solve the Great Emergency. If you could put one person into a harmonically induced suspended animation, who would it be? (We will not accept the answer "My annoying brother/sister.")

4.   When Victor, Scott, and Benjamin Franklin needed to create a lightning storm in order to save Philadelphia, they asked weatherman Skip Weaver for advice. If you had to create a tornado to save a major metropolitan city, how would you go about doing it? What if you had to create an earthquake? A citywide blanket of soupy fog?

5.   If the people running the Modern Order of Prometheus created a secret training program for new Custodians disguised as a fake online business, what do you think they would call their Web site?